NextWorld

Super Science Fiction Stories

JOHN WHITMAN

ROXBURY PARK

LOWELL HOUSE JUVENILE

LOS ANGELES

NTC/Contemporary Publishing Group

Published by Lowell House
A division of NTC/Contemporary Publishing Group, Inc.
4255 West Touhy Avenue, Lincolnwood (Chicago), Illinois 60712-1975 U.S.A.

Lowell House books can be purchased at special discounts when ordered in bulk for premiums and special sales. Contact Department CS at the following address:
NTC/Contemporary Publishing Group
4255 West Touhy Avenue
Lincolnwood, IL 60712-1975
1-800-323-4900

ISBN: 0-7373-0503-7
Library of Congress Control Number: 00-133245

Roxbury Park is a division of NTC/Contemporary Publishing Group, Inc.

Managing Director and Publisher: Jack Artenstein
Editor in Chief, Roxbury Park Books: Michael Artenstein
Director of Publishing Services: Rena Copperman
Senior Editor: Maria Magallanes
Editorial Assistant: Nicole Monastirsky
Cover Art: Scott Grimando
Interior Design: Anna Christian

Printed and bound in the United States of America
00 01 02 DHD 10 9 8 7 6 5 4 3 2 1

Contents

The Magic Fish

Langostino Tregor knew he was going insane, but that was the least of his worries.

His star freighter was adrift in space, a thousand light years from any civilized planet. His life support systems had shut down, he was running out of air, and his only companion onboard was his mechanical copilot, the automate ZDE-X, or Dex for short.

"Technically," said Dex, shuffling on mechanical legs toward the pilot's seat where Langostino slumped, "you're not going insane. It's simply oxygen deprivation. Your brain isn't getting enough air, so you're starting to hallucinate."

"I don't care what you call it," the young space trader said, "I'm nuts. The control panels just turned into fish."

He wasn't kidding. He'd been staring at the control panels in the cockpit of his ship, trying to find some way to restore power. But the air was growing so thin he found it hard to focus his eyes—or his brain. His vision blurred and the controls began to swim in front of him. The instant the word *swim* popped into his brain, the controls turned into fish and wriggled right through the viewport of his ship and out into space.

"Yep, I'm nuts," he said out loud.

"You have no one to blame but yourself," Dex said. Although programmed to mimic human behavior, even human thought, Dex was still a machine. Hidden from view underneath his pseudoskin was a network of microprocessors, servomotors, and other wonders of 23rd-century technology. And since breathing wasn't one of the requirements for being a machine, the automate was doing just fine in the vacuum of space.

"Really?" Langostino gasped. "I blame you."

"Me?" The artificial humanoid put one hand to his chest.

"Yeah. You forgot to tell me the Screpulousians could scan for faulty fusion cores."

Dex looked slightly annoyed. "But I'm not the one who sold fake fusion cores to the natives of Screpulous 3. I'm not the one who provoked chase by Screpulousian battle cruisers, resulting in our engines getting shot out from under us and our being left here for dead, with no oxygen."

More fish materialized on the console and swam out into the ocean of stars. Langostino scoffed, "What do you care about oxygen? It's loss is going to kill me, not you."

"True," Dex said. "But then I'll be stuck on this derelict ship forever with no one to talk to. So I say you're getting off easy."

If there'd been enough air in the cabin, Langostino would have sighed. There was no arguing with a model X automate.

They were programmed to think logically and, Langostino was convinced, to win every argument.

"I'm too young to die," he rasped. "I'm only 17! Plus I've got two billion credits in the cargo hold."

More imaginary fish swam out into space.

"You know, this whole thing reminds me of the story of the magic fish," Langostino said weakly. "You know that story?"

There was a whir as Dex checked his hard drive. "No."

"It's about a fisherman who never catches anything. One day he tries so hard he gets lost at sea. But he manages to catch the most beautiful fish he's ever seen. This fish can talk. It says to him, 'I'm a magic fish. I'll grant you a wish, anything you want in the whole world, as long as you let me go.' "

"I see," said Dex, sounding bored. "What did the man wish for?"

Langostino laughed. "He said, 'I want to be the richest man in the world!' The fish said, 'Done! Your wish is granted. Now let me go!' The man let him go and the fish splashed back into the water."

Dex made a sound like a human sigh. "Ah. But the man was still lost at sea."

Langostino groaned. "Yeah."

"What happened next?" Dex asked.

Langostino shrugged. His thoughts were becoming muddled. The air in the cabin was almost gone. "There's more, but I can't really remember it right now . . ."

Just then the ship shuddered as if grabbed by a giant hand. The transponder bleeped and a voice blared over the speakers:

"Attention, alien vessel! We are the Klahr! You have entered our systems without permission. You are in violation!"

"Oh, drak," Langostino groaned. "Not the Klahr."

The Klahr were an alien species that had almost no contact with humans or any other life-form in the galaxy. Very few people had actually seen them, but everyone had heard of them. The Klahr were notorious—they believed they were far superior to every other living thing in the galaxy. They viewed other races as brainless, undeserving of slithering out of the oceans let alone flying among the stars.

The voice blared again. "Prepare to be boarded."

Langostino gulped. The Klahr weren't known for their hospitality.

—

Prime Number Angulus Rood sat back in his command node. When he stood straight, as he usually did when commanding his patrol ship, Rood was nearly six and a half feet tall. But at the moment, satisfied with the way his crew had spotted and picked up the trading ship so quickly, he allowed himself to relax. The Klahrs' instruments had reported the ship damaged and disabled. Nevertheless, Operating Rules stated that every trespasser be treated as hostile and, like all Klahr, Rood was a stickler for rules.

"Prime Number?" asked a subordinate, stepping up to Rood's node.

"Yes, Number One?" the commander replied, straightening up.

"The alien vessel is safely in the cargo hold, and our Forcible Entry Team is standing by."

"Excellent," the Prime Number said, stepping out of his module. Around him, the bridge of his ship hummed with activity. All was orderly—not a single crewmember out of position, not a single wrinkle on a uniform. Just the way Prime Number Rood liked it.

Rood marched toward the transportube, his Number One falling in behind him. Once they were both inside, the commander said crisply, "Holding bay," and the tube whisked them through the ship to the appropriate spot. The doors snapped open, and Rood found himself in the vaultlike cargo hold. Inside sat a squat, ugly ship, like a lump dropped by a guano beast.

Rood felt the nostril sacs in his nose puff up in disdain. Like all decent Klahr, he detested imprecision, and this junk heap looked like it had been thrown together. A squad of Klahr soldiers with laser weapons stood at attention. As Rood approached, one of them stepped forward on legs that were long and spindly, even for a Klahr.

"Sir!" the Klahr soldier said. "The exterior of the ship has been checked out from stem to stern, sir! It poses no threat. There's evidence of heavy damage from some sort of battle. Logic indicates that is why it drifted into our space."

Rood studied the ship. The hull of the small freighter was certainly marked with blaster fire. But the Prime Number didn't believe it for a nanosecond. "The oldest trick in the manual, Number One," he chided. "Make it appear as though they've escaped our enemies and are therefore our friends. A pathetic attempt at espionage. Bring the creature out."

Two soldiers marched up to the ship's hull, found the entry hatch, and pressed a small device to the exterior. The device forced a transmitter signal through the hull, overriding the ship's security system. A second later the hatch opened.

"Move! Move! Move!" shouted the squad leader. The Klahr rushed into the ship.

—

Langostino heard them coming, but there was nothing he could do. Or wanted to, actually. He was just relieved to be breathing again. The minute the Klahr had sucked his ship into theirs, he'd been able to open the vents and gulp fresh air. Now feeling light-headed from too much oxygen, all he could do when the Klahr burst into his cabin was smile. "Hi, fellas," he said before they pinched his arms and dragged him out of the ship.

The young trader didn't get a clear look at a Klahr until he was dropped unceremoniously at the feet of the one who was in charge. He looked up . . . and up . . . until his eyes located what appeared to be the face of the ship commander.

It took a moment to get used to looking at the Klahr, though at first Langostino couldn't figure out why. Then he realized the creature was made entirely of straight lines and angles. There wasn't a curve anywhere on its body. Its head was a triangle. Its eye sockets were shaped like diamonds. It didn't seem to have a neck—just a long body that appeared to swivel back and forth on multiple joints. Instead of skin, the creature was wrapped in a tight, hard shell, like a bug.

In its face, two slits flared open, then subsided in an expression of disgust. The Klahr said, "You are human."

"Yes, sir, captain," Langostino said nervously. The cold glint in the creature's eyes made the young trader think that suffocating in space might not have been so bad after all.

"You are also a trespasser. You have violated Klahr space, which means that you are clearly a spy. We are going to question you. Then we'll kill you."

—

"But I'm not a spy!"

Langostino had shouted the phrase a dozen times as they dragged him to a detention cell, and he'd yelled it a dozen more from behind the transparent restraining shield that kept him locked in the tiny room.

The room itself seemed to have been designed for optimum discomfort. It was all sharp edges and flat, hard surfaces.

Suddenly, Prime Number Rood stepped into view, flanked by two Klahr with laser rifles—and Dex. The Klahr deactivated the restraining shield and pushed Dex into the cell. The energy screen dropped down instantly.

"Hey, Dex!" Langostino said, genuinely happy. "Where've you been?"

The Prime Number said, "We have already interrogated your companion. He is surprisingly intelligent for one of your species."

"One of my—?" Langostino started to say.

"He lacks all of your species' irrational behavior and speech. He is logical. A credit to your race."

"They don't make 'em any better, that's for sure," Langostino said sarcastically.

He looked at Dex. To his eyes, the automate clearly wasn't human. Although Dex's skin and hair were carefully crafted to appear natural, there wasn't a man, woman, or child on earth who couldn't have picked him out as a machine. Stiff and awkward as his movements were, it was in fact his lack of movement that gave him away. Like any other machine, Dex had the unnerving ability to sit completely still when not in use. Langostino had seem him sit, without twitching the tiniest servo in his pseudoskin, for hours.

"For a moment we considered that he might not be human," Rood continued, "but his explanation for your presence in our space is illogical."

"What did you say?" Langostino asked, worried about the fortune he had stuffed in his cargo bay.

Dex blinked at him. "The truth, naturally. I said that you were a chronic liar and a thief who had sold faulty goods to other members of your species. These others then attacked you and left you for dead out in space, where your ship drifted off course."

The young trader nodded. "Yeah, that's about it."

Prime Number Rood swiveled his triangular head. "That story has too many logical flaws. First, no intelligent species preys on itself, so you could not possibly have tried to pass off poor equipment to your own kind."

Oh, yeah? thought Langostino. *A guy'll do a lot for two billion credits!*

"Second, if you were attacked by members of your own species, they would not have left you alive, even in space. That would be illogical."

"Those rascals," Langostino said.

"And finally, the chances of you drifting into our space on the cusp of our Earth invasion are preposterous."

The young trader's jaw nearly dropped. "Um . . . did you say 'invasion'?"

"Of course," the Klahr said with a wave of his angular hand. "Pretending ignorance is a waste of time. Our battle fleet has just dropped out of quantum drive to these coordinates. Clearly you knew this."

"He's not joking," Dex said. "I saw the fleet from the viewport. Several thousand ships, including a Juggernaut."

Langostino's blood turned ice-cold. Juggernauts were the most feared battleships in the galaxy—death-dealing automated planet-killers that, once activated, could not be stopped. Most planetary fleets didn't even have them. They were notoriously difficult to program as well as dangerous to control once their fusion cores had been powered up.

The Klahr Prime Number nodded. "Obviously your attempt at espionage has failed. I'll give you 10 minutes to consider your plight logically. When I return, if you have not agreed to tell me everything you know about our plans, you will be wrapped in a needle blanket and dumped into an antigravity chamber."

The alien commander pivoted sharply on his thin legs and ambled away.

"I wish I knew something," the trader groaned. "I'd tell them in an instant."

"Ah, human courage in the face of danger," Dex said with a snicker.

Hey, you're not the one who's going to get the needle blanket," Langostino said with a shudder. "Whatever that is."

"It sounds unpleasant," his mechanical cohort admitted.

"I can't believe they think I'm a spy," the human said. "It's ridiculous."

"Utterly," Dex agreed. "But my data banks have some information on the Klahr. They are incapable of illogical thinking. Therefore your illogical explanations are unbelievable to them."

"But all humans are illogical!" Langostino protested.

Dex nodded. "Hence the invasion."

The trader glared. "Whose side are you on, anyway?"

The automate said, "Yours. Otherwise, I wouldn't do this."

And with that, Dex walked through the restraint barrier that locked Langostino in the cell.

The trader jumped back, expecting the sizzle that usually accompanied the disintegration of a living object zapped by restraint barriers. But nothing happened.

"Hey!" was all Langostino could say.

Dex gave the mechanical equivalent of a shrug. "The energy field is set to a certain density that prohibits the passage of living flesh. Heavier things, though, can go through. Therefore guards can pass prisoners behind the barrier such items as bowls of food."

Dex stepped out of view for a moment, and Langostino heard him entering code into an access panel. A second later the energy field dropped completely.

"What now?" the trader asked as he stepped out of the cell.

"I suggest we run for the ship. It's the only way out."

Langostino started to run, but Dex grabbed his shoulder. "Walking is more advisable in this instance."

The human and his automate walked down the hall. Dex took the lead, since his computer brain could easily retrace their path back to the cargo bay. To Langostino's surprise, they met no resistance. They passed several Klahr in the corridors, but none tried to stop the escapees.

"I don't get it—" the trader started to say.

"It's simple logic," the automate interrupted. "If we were running, it would be logical to assume that something was wrong, and the logical response would be to detain us. However, because we're walking free, it's logical to assume that we're allowed to walk free. Therefore no one bothers us."

The escapees stepped into a transportube. The doors closed and it hummed into motion.

"This is a piece of cake," Langostino said with a laugh. "We just let these Klahr keep applying logic to everything, while we use good ol' human ingenuity." He laughed as the transportube slowed and the doors opened. "No contest!"

Then Prime Number Rood shot him in the chest.

—

Langostino felt the stun bolt slam like an asteroid into his breastbone. Instantly his knees turned to water and he dropped to the ground, gasping for breath. Before he could even think about moving, two Klahr soldiers pulled him to his feet to face the Prime Number.

Rood puffed his nostril sacs in disdain. "Idiot. Returning to your ship was the logical and therefore predictable thing to do."

Langostino tried to respond but he couldn't get his mouth to work. Finally, he mumbled, "Needle blanket then?"

Rood considered. "No. Current data has changed my conclusion. Bring him."

The Klahr dragged Langostino out into the middle of the cargo bay. Dex, watched closely by two more soldiers, followed passively. The soldiers released the trader, and he slumped down next to a large metal object he vaguely recognized.

As the stun bolt wore off he focused his watery eyes and saw that it was his last fusion core—the one he never sold because it was real and in good working order. That single fusion core was the bait in his bait-and-switch scheme. He used the core to prove his merchandise was good, then handed over his faulty cores when it came time to deliver. It was a scheme that had worked for him a dozen times—until he'd met the Screpulousians.

"Is that what I think it is?" the Prime Number demanded.

"Yup," Langostino nodded. "I wish I'd never seen it."

"You should reconsider that opinion," the Klahr said. "This fusion core has just saved your life."

Langostino gasped audibly. "Excuse me?"

"This device confirms your story," Rood explained. "No government would send a spy carrying exactly the equipment the enemy needs."

"Excuse me?" Langostino said again.

"The fusion core," Dex piped up. "If memory serves, it is exactly what the Klahr need to power their Juggernaut."

"Yeah, but I can't let you—" Langostino started to say. Then he caught himself.

Stars and planets, Tregor, he said to himself, *you must really be slipping. First you let yourself get nabbed by the Screpulousians, and now you nearly miss a stellar opportunity like this.*

"Well, yes," he said. "By all means, you can have it. Just let me go."

"Clearly," the Prime Number concluded, "you are what you say. The Earth defenses could not have known we needed a fusion core, so these cannot be part of some sabotage plot. It is merely our good fortune."

"So can I go?" Langostino asked hopefully.

"No. We need you to install this fusion core for us. The designs are different from ours. Only if you perform the task well will we let you live."

———

Four hours later, Langostino Tregor and Dex were crawling through a tiny service tube that led to the engine room of the Juggernaut. The core itself had been inserted into the Juggernaut's colossal engines. Now Langostino carried a command chip that had to be installed at a relay station. Beside him Dex carried a kit of delicate tools that would be used to manipulate the relay's microchips. The work had so far been difficult, dirty, and dangerous, and Langostino was fairly sure he'd been exposed to unhealthy doses of radiation. But a visit to an atomic clinic could fix that—once he was free and clear of the Klahr.

"We're almost out of here," he said for the 20th time. "Just finish installing this and—"

"Yes, yes, and we'll put light years between us and them," Dex intoned. "I heard you the first time."

"Well excuse me for gloating," the trader said, finding the proper access panel and popping it open. Behind lay the most organized and neatly planned cross section of wires he'd ever seen. The Klahr were insane about order. "But it's not often a kid like me gets to outwit the Screpulousians and escape the Klahr on the same day."

Dex raised the artificial hair that passed for an eyebrow. "Is that what you call outwitting the Screpulousians? They nearly blasted the ship into its atomic elements."

"Details, details," Langostino murmured as he worked.

"And we are hardly escaping the Klahr," the automate said sternly. "In fact, I feel obligated to point out that you are endangering billions of lives by installing this fusion core. Once the Juggernaut is activated, it will be nearly impossible for Earth's defenses to withstand it."

Langostino growled, "One problem at a time."

"The next problem could mean the destruction of an entire world," Dex pointed out.

"And this problem could mean I get killed!" Langostino snapped. "If I don't do what they ask, the Klahr will disintegrate me without a thought."

Dex frowned. "Sir, you know I'm programmed for service, and I've considered it my duty to follow you on even your most unscrupulous ventures. But this . . ." the machine shook its humanlike head. "This is beyond even my tolerance levels."

Dex dropped the tool kit he was holding.

"C'mon, Dex," Langostino said. "It's not like I have any choice!"

No response.

"Dex," Langostino said sternly. "I want you to help me with this. That's an order."

Still no response.

Langostino groaned inwardly. Normally an automate's program wouldn't allow it to disobey a direct order from its programmer. But Dex had found a loophole in his programming. Putting some lives—well, *billions* of lives—in danger violated the automate's prime directive, which was to preserve and enhance human life.

"Dex!"

The mechanical creature stood as still as a statue, his eyes staring blankly into Langostino's. The automate had retreated somewhere into the depths of his programming and, the trader realized, could stand there for a thousand years before he moved another servo.

"Fine then!" the trader spat in disgust. "You're no good to me here. Go back and prep the ship. The Klahr will release us as soon as I'm done."

Dex shifted out of his frozen mode and allowed the hint of a sneer to cross his synthetic face. "As you wish."

The automate turned to leave, looking even stiffer than usual. Langostino glared at his back until Dex was out of sight. The minute the automate was gone, Langostino felt terribly alone.

The truth was, Dex was the only companion he'd had for more than a week or two. Most of his "friends" were other con artists and scam runners. They joined up with him when it suited their needs and dumped him like trash when his usefulness was done. Although he was a machine, Dex was more human than most of the humans he knew.

Langostino hesitated for a moment, his eyes chasing in vain after the departed automate. Then, with a heavy hand, he picked up the tools and continued his work.

—

Prime Number Rood waited impatiently as his soldiers escorted the human back into the cargo bay. He glowered at the trader, "Your work is complete?" he snapped.

The human nodded. "The fusion core's been installed. It's ready to go. Can I return to my ship now?"

"Not so fast," the Klahr said, gripping his arm. With his free hand, the Prime Number plucked a transmitter from his belt and spoke into it. "Bridge, this is Prime Number Rood. Run a start test on the Juggernaut's engine."

Rood watched the alien closely as a voice responded from the bridge, "Affirmative, sir."

A moment later there was a low rumble beneath their feet. Somewhere inside the vast Juggernaut, massive engines shook themselves awake, then died down with a shudder.

The voice spoke through the transmitter. "All indicators show optimum, sir. The core is now active, engines on idle."

Rood nodded. "You are free to leave," he said tersely. "Although I do not think returning to Earth would be your most logical choice."

—

Langostino climbed heavily into the cockpit of his ship. Dex was sitting in the copilot's seat. He'd already fed a launch pattern into the computer.

The automate stared at his controls. "We've been given clearance to leave. In fact, we've been ordered to leave. The Klahr fleet is preparing a hyperlight thrust straight to Earth," he reported.

Langostino simply replied, "Is the ship ready?"

Dex nodded, still not looking at Langostino. "The damage was not extensive. The Klahr repaired it quickly. We won't win any hyperlight speed records, but the ship moves."

"Good. Activate thrusters and get us out of here as soon as possible."

Dex punched a command into the guidance computer. The frail freighter groaned, grumbled, and lifted off the cargo bay deck. A set of massive doors opened into the emptiness of space and the freighter slid forward, escaping from the Klahr Juggernaut like a fly out of a crocodile's open jaws moments before they snapped.

"Any chance of getting us up to hyperlight speed?" Langostino asked.

"No," Dex replied. "She's at maximum now."

The trader sighed. "Well, just put as much distance between us and them as you can."

"What's your hurry? *They'll* be leaving in a few seconds."

"Not really."

For the first time, Dex looked at Langostino. "What?"

"Watch," the trader said.

Dex swung the damaged star freighter around until the entire Klahr fleet came into view. It was the first time Langostino had really seen it. There must have been over a thousand ships, stretching as far as he could see, nearly blotting out the stars. And in the center of the swarm lumbered the enormous Juggernaut, big as a moon.

Without warning, a quantum laser bolt flashed from one of the Juggernaut's thousand batteries and obliterated the nearest Klahr ship. Then another laser flashed and another and still another. In seconds the Juggernaut was firing so many weapons that it glowed like a star. And each time it fired, a Klahr ship vanished.

The Klahr fleet was slow to react. At first, squads of ships simply hovered, dumbfounded. But then someone, probably Prime Number Rood, must have given an order. The ships scattered, trying to evade the Juggernaut's weapons system. They even returned fire. In seconds, an intense battle was raging.

"What—?" Dex asked Langostino, who shrugged. "What did you do?"

The trader gave a half smile. "Once I'd installed the fusion core, the logical thing for Rood to do was check it to make sure it worked. So I tweaked the Juggernaut's programming a bit. I programmed its weapons system to start up a few minutes after the engines test-fired."

Dex managed to look both stunned and impressed at the same time. "And since Juggernauts are notoriously difficult to program in any case—"

"—the Klahr won't be able to shut it down until most of their fleet's wiped out."

"I am impressed," Dex admitted.

An alarm bleeped, and Langostino glanced down at a tactical display. Then he said, "Hey, I never did tell you the end of that magic fish story."

"No," Dex said almost cheerfully. "You can tell me while I pilot the ship to the nearest spaceport."

"Don't bother," Langostino said. "Sit back, relax." The trader spared one more glance at the display on the control board, then eased himself back into his seat.

"So the fisherman lets the fish go and realizes he may be the richest man in the world, but he's still lost at sea. Growing desperate, he fishes for food to stay alive. And wouldn't you know, he catches the same fish!"

"A strange coincidence," Dex said. The automate was clearly confused by Langostino's behavior. Then he noticed the readout Langostino had been studying. It showed a squadron of Klahr fighters. They'd broken off from the main group and were streaking toward them at attack speed.

Langostino continued. "So once the fisherman has the fish again, the fish naturally says, 'Look, I'm still a magic fish! If you let me go, I'll grant you another wish!'"

Dex realized what his friend already knew: There was no way for them to outrun Klahr fighters. He sat back too. "And what did the fisherman ask for?"

"Nothing," Langostino said. "He ate the fish."

Together they watched the fighters come into firing range.

Long-Distance Call

The ghostly image of the murderer loomed over the victim, both bodies outlined by the dim light of a street lamp.

Gina Lombard peeked around the corner of the alley, watching the horrible scene play out. She knew she shouldn't be there. But a horrible fascination gripped her. She couldn't pull herself away.

A heavy hand fell on her shoulder. "What are you doing here?"

Gina whirled around and found herself looking into a tough, grizzled face that was all too familiar.

"Dad!" she yelled. "You scared me!"

Her father, Detective Bart Lombard, frowned. "Serves you right," he said wearily. "What are you doing here? You know crime scenes are off-limits."

Gina shrugged. "Sorry, Dad. I heard on the webcast that there'd been a murder here, and I figured you'd show up."

Detective Lombard shook his head. "You're going to make a great detective some day, Gina, but dark alleys are no place for a 13-year-old. What's your mother going to say?"

Gina swallowed. "Well . . . nothing, if we don't tell her. She won't be back from grandma's until Sunday. Besides, it's not a school night or anything. Tomorrow's Saturday."

Her father checked his watch. "Well, let's get you back home before anything else happens. I'm about done here anyway."

"Oh please, can I look at the mood ring? Please?"

The detective groaned. "If I don't say yes, I'll hear about it all the way home. All right, let's go."

Excitedly, Gina hurried toward the crowd of police huddled around the crime scene. At its border, someone had set up a tripod with a sensor on top and as she approached, the sensor scanned her. Failing to find a police badge or ID transmitter on her anywhere, the sensor barked, "Halt! You are approaching a crime scene! No admittance. Halt! You are approaching a crime scene! No adm—*squawk!*"

The recording fell silent as Detective Lombard strode forward and reset it. At the sound of the alarm, several of the police officers turned toward the disturbance. Seeing Gina they quickly lost interest. Most of them worked the same beat as Detective Lombard, and they recognized his daughter.

Gina Lombard had a passion for police work for as long as she could remember. As a baby she'd loved the sound of hovercar sirens. As she grew older, she preferred her father's stories of crimes he'd solved to fairy tales. And now that she was old enough to take autocab rides around the city, she found crime scenes irresistible. Any time her father was called on a case, she had to be there. Unsolved mysteries were like an itch she just had to scratch.

There was, however, one thing Gina loved as much as a mystery: living in the Tech Age, which is what people were calling the 22nd Century. New devices and new uses for technology popped up almost every day. There hadn't been such a technology explosion since the computer was invented back in the 20th century.

Computers, of course, were ancient history for Gina. What interested her presently was a small circular device lying on the ground in the middle of the alley. From that device, a lens projected the ghostly image of the murderer and his victim.

The 3-D projection was terrifyingly real. The murderer bent over his victim, hands around the other man's throat. Now motionless as a still photo, the victim clearly had flailed around, trying desperately to get away. Even frozen in time, the image conveyed sheer terror.

The device's technical name was the Residual Imager, but most people called it the "mood ring" because of how it worked.

Scientists had known for years that the human body gives off energy. Search teams used heat-sensitive sensors to locate missing hikers in the wilderness. Doctors mapped bioelectric impulses to locate brain tumors and other illnesses. Researchers had even learned to read the "aura" of a person—the energy a person's body gives off, especially when seized by strong emotions.

Then a few years ago a scientist named Wolfgang Ruger proved that not only did people give off energy but also that no two people had the same energy field. It was, Dr. Ruger explained, like a fingerprint. He dubbed his discovery the energy print, and he invented a device called the Residual Imager to read the energy prints that people left behind. But since the device worked best when strong emotions had been displayed, everyone else called it the mood ring.

Law enforcement quickly put the mood ring to use. After all, it could identify a criminal just by taking a reading of a crime scene. Because of its link to intense emotion, the mood ring was a perfect tool for detectives like Gina's dad, who investigated violent crimes.

The device had only one drawback. It could only read energy prints left behind within 24 hours. So if the crime wasn't discovered until much later, the mood ring was useless.

In amazement, Gina studied the holographic image projected by this mood ring.

"Pretty amazing, huh?" her father said, mirroring her expression.

Gina nodded. "Yeah."

A technician appeared beside her father.

"Detective, I've got bad news for you," the techie said.

"Spill it," her father sighed.

"It looks like we got here too late. This is as good as the resolution's going to get," the man said. "And without a more detailed readout, we can't match it up with anyone in WETworks."

Gina and her father both glanced up at the holographic image. Although the outline of the figure was very clear, the details were fuzzy. The face wasn't much more than a blob, which meant the mood ring couldn't read 100 percent of the energy signature. The device used the signature to match up the readout with the international database known as WETworks—the Worldwide Energy Tag workstation. It was exactly like the old FBI's fingerprint files a few hundred years ago.

"Figures," Detective Lombard groaned. "Gina, I've got to go inside for a minute. Wait right here."

The detective strode off, his trench coat swirling behind him.

The techie watched Lombard stride away. "So that's the famous Detective Lombard, huh?"

"I don't know about famous," Gina said. "He's just my dad."

"Your dad's the guy who tracked down Damien Blackchurch?"

Gina nodded. She knew about the case, of course. Damien Blackchurch had been on the Global Most Wanted List for years, but no one could find him until Detective Lombard took the case. Blackchurch tried to escape aboard a stolen space shuttle, but Detective Lombard chased him all the way to Saturn. Blackchurch met his end trying to fly through Saturn's rings, where his ship disintegrated.

The techie whistled. "Man, that was one great piece of detective work. But you know, they never found his body. He could still be alive. In fact, this nasty piece of work here looks like his kind of job." The techie pointed to the image of the throttled victim.

Gina shuddered. Blackchurch had been one of the worst criminals ever. And before disappearing, he'd sworn revenge on Gina's father. She didn't want to think about what he'd do if he were alive.

"Well," the techie said comfortingly. "I bet your dad's got nothing to worry about with you around, Miss Lombard. You gonna solve this case for him?"

Gina said, "I could if the mood ring read older signatures."

"Well," the techie said. "If you come up with a way to make the mood ring work better, we'll solve this case in a snap!"

Gina's father appeared, looking tired and grim. "All right, boys, pack it up. We've got what we can here, and we've already interviewed everyone within 10 blocks of the place. That's all we can do for now."

"Yes, sir," said the techie. "You signed the mood ring out. Do you want to return it tonight?"

Detective Lombard frowned. "Can you drive it back to the station for me?"

The techie shook his head. "Sorry, sir. Regulations. You signed it out, you have to return it."

The detective checked his watch. "Not tonight. I'll take it home and turn it back in on Monday."

The drive home seemed short to Gina but much longer to her father, who had to field a dozen questions from her about detective work. His eyelids were drooping by the time their air-car pulled into the driveway, and he looked like he could fall asleep on his feet when they walked into the house.

And then the holophone in the living room buzzed. "Oh, what?" Detective Lombard groaned. He clicked on the small device.

Instantly the miniature image of a police dispatcher appeared. Gina's father straightened up a bit, knowing that somewhere in an office downtown, his own image was appearing as a hologram on her desk, just as her three-dimensional image appeared in front of him.

"Detective Lombard, please report to the corner of Fifth Street and Angelotti Avenue," the dispatcher said.

"What's the call?" he asked.

The dispatcher looked down, checking a readout on her desk. "Assault at a bar."

Lombard shook his head. "Oh man, I gotta find a new job," he said. "Okay, you go to bed, Gina. I'll be out all night now."

Her father dropped the mood ring onto the coffee table and went out.

—

There was just no way Gina was going to sleep. An hour after she'd crawled into bed, she was still wide awake, thinking about the mood ring.

If you come up with a way to make the mood ring work better, we'll solve this case in a snap. That's what the techie had said.

Gina reviewed all the things she knew about the mood ring. She had what her father called "a real brain" for technology. Every article on the Datanet about the mood ring and its inventor, Dr. Wolfgang Ruger, she'd not only read but also understood. Now she mentally revisited those articles as she lay awake.

And then it struck her.

She knew how to do it.

At least she thought she did. There was only one way to find out . . . and that involved taking a device that didn't really belong to her.

Gina was part police detective's daughter, and that part of her said clearly, "Don't do it."

But Gina was also part adventurer, part inventor, and part mystery-solver. And that made three to one.

—

Once she thought about it, the solution was obvious. So obvious, in fact, that no one had considered it. The first rule of detective work was that the simplest answer was probably the right one. But detectives sometimes got so caught up in the twists and turns of a case that they missed the plain truth. It was the same with scientists, Gina guessed. They got so involved in the most intricate details of their experiments, they sometimes overlooked the simplest solution.

The simple solution that Gina found was in her own living room. In fact, it was in the living room of every single person on the planet.

It was the holophone.

After all, the holophone used signal boosters and buffers to clear up images sent over very long distances as well as to clarify holograms transmitted over weak links. If she could just reprogram it to boost the signal created by the mood ring, it might be able to read older vibrations.

To Gina's surprise, the reprogramming didn't take her long at all. Her father had always told her that solving mysteries was like solving puzzles. It all looked confusing at first, but once you started down the right path, the pieces just seemed to fall into place.

Still, it was very late by the time she was done. The sun was just coming up as she stepped back and surveyed her work. With its casing on, the mood ring didn't look any different, but inside the device had been totally reconstructed. And it was now successfully wired to the holophone.

Gina had been up all night, and she knew she ought to be exhausted. But instead she felt elated. She was sure her solution would work. But how to test it?

Gina couldn't go back to the crime scene she'd visited earlier—it might still be crawling with policemen. There was only one other crime scene that Gina knew about.

Making her decision quickly, she snatched up the mood ring and holophone, packed them into a backpack, and dashed out the door.

—

The spaceport was a brief taxi ride away. Fortunately there were enough family travelers at the port to allow Gina to blend in. She walked down one of the runway ramps to Gate 32. It had been here, not too long ago, that her father had tracked down the notorious Blackchurch just as the criminal attempted his getaway. This is where the famous "chase into space" had begun.

Again fortunately, no flights were leaving from Gate 32 at that moment, so Gina had the place to herself. She set up the mood ring, wires still connecting it to the holophone.

The young detective activated the mood ring and began to scroll through its database. Since the mood ring had a direct link to WETworks, it could access the energy print of everyone the devices had ever scanned. It would read energy signals in the area and try to match them with prints in its data banks.

Gina activated her makeshift device. The first holographic image that popped up was of a woman. She looked like she was crying. The screen on the device bleeped, and the words *No match* came up.

Gina looked at the image of the woman and felt a tug at her heart. The woman looked so sad. Her arm was waving good-bye. She was probably seeing a loved one off on a space flight.

But that didn't tell Gina what she needed to know. The woman could have been at the launch gate early that morning or late last night. She pressed *Cycle* on the mood ring and it began to automatically sort through energy signals, looking for ones it could match. Gina watched a whole parade of people appear before her: tall, short, fat, skinny, young, old. The people were either crying or yelling or, in a few cases, laughing hysterically. Again, the mood ring worked best with strong emotions.

Suddenly the mood ring stopped cycling, and the monitor bleeped. The word *Match* appeared. Gina looked up at the image.

Staring down at her was a tall man with broad shoulders and a hard, square face. He wasn't laughing or crying. His mouth was set in a grim expression, and Gina understood instantly what emotion he was feeling. Hatred. This man clearly hated everyone and everything.

Gina looked down at the name on the screen, but she knew what it would be. *Blackchurch.*

She was looking at an image of the infamous Damien Blackchurch. But it had been almost two months since her father had been on the Blackchurch case. She'd done it! Her enhanced mood ring had picked up the energy signal of a man who hadn't been in the area for almost 60 days!

Gina was so excited, she ran for the nearest holophone. She had to tell someone! She sprinted down the hallway and around a corner, but found the three holophone boths occupied. She waitied a moment before she realized that she'd left the device itself back by the gate. Instantly she turned and sprinted back.

To her relief the mood ring was still where she'd left it. But it had been turned off, and the image of Blackchurch was gone. Standing beside the device was a young boy about six. His mother sat in a chair nearby, reading the morning news on her handheld digital display.

"Please don't touch that," Gina said. "It's fragile."

The boy stepped back, startled. "I didn't," he said. "Honest, I didn't touch it."

Gina smiled to show that she wasn't too upset. "How'd it get turned off then?"

The little boy shrugged. "Maybe the man did it. There was a man here before me."

Gina raised an eyebrow. She hadn't seen anyone. But it didn't matter. The mood ring wasn't broken, and that was the important thing. She gave the little boy one more smile, gathered up the mood ring and holophone in her backpack, and ran back to the taxi stand.

The taxi ride home didn't lessen any of her excitement. She had to tell someone. But who? None of her friends were into police work or technology, so none of them would care. She could tell her father, but then she'd have to admit tinkering with a device that belonged to the government (not to mention staying up all night).

There was only one person she could tell. It was crazy to call him, but she'd read enough about him to know he was pretty eccentric himself.

She would call Dr. Ruger.

And she could do it right now, using the holophone there in her backpack.

Without hesitating, she activated the holophone and dialed information, accessing the Global Holo Network. Usually, the Network brought up any bit of information instantly, but for some reason it hummed this time, sorting through databanks of information until finally the name of Dr. Ruger popped onto the holophone's small screen. He was listed! Gina punched in the number and waited another moment.

As the holophone made its connection, an image appeared, but to Gina's surprise it appeared not on the holophone but on the mood ring. She'd forgotten that the two devices were still attached.

In the hazy light of the mood ring's projector, Gina saw the image of a man's head. The man looked utterly bewildered.

Probably surprised that anyone would call him this early, Gina thought.

"What—what is it?" the doctor asked.

"Dr. Ruger," Gina began, "you don't know me but my name is Gina Lombard. I'm sorry to call you like this."

"Well, it certainly is a surprise," the doctor replied.

"It's just that I have news that couldn't wait. I've done something remarkable."

"You most certainly have," Dr. Ruger agreed, "getting in touch with me like this."

Gina blushed. Was he insulting her for being rude? Well, she couldn't help herself, and she was too excited to stop now. "I've managed to boost the mood ring's signal! I think it can pick up weaker images now!"

A look of understanding passed over the doctor's face. "Ah, I see! That explains this call. Why, that's wonderful, my child!" Dr. Ruger grinned. "You have done something no one else in the world has been able to do!"

Gina blushed again. "It really wasn't all that much, I just—"

"But you must listen to me," Dr. Ruger said suddenly. His eyes seemed to stare right into her. "You are in grave danger!"

"Danger?" Gina said in confusion. "What do you mean?"

"You've opened a door into something that cannot be easily explained . . ." Dr. Ruger shook his head and stopped himself. "No, wait. This is all happening so suddenly. I need time to know what to do. Call me again tonight."

The image disappeared.

—

Gina reached home, not knowing what to think. What had Dr. Ruger meant by danger? And from whom?

Gina walked into her house. "Hello?" It was no use trying

to enter quietly. Her father had returned from his case and had discovered her missing or else he wasn't home yet. Either way, there was no reason to sneak in.

No answer came, but she heard noises from the kitchen. She walked in but found the lights off. The kitchen was lit only by the dim bulb activated by the open refrigerator door, and even that was blocked by her father, his back to her as he stared at what was inside. The pale light cast an eery glow over his back, giving her the impression that he was glowing.

Gina gulped. Her dad must *really* be mad at her not to answer her greeting. He hadn't even turned to look at her yet.

"Um, Dad, is everything okay?"

"Sure," came the muffled reply from the refrigerator. He stood up and whirled around to glare at her. "Everything is just fine."

Gina froze. The man staring down at her wasn't her father. It was someone she had just seen.

Blackchurch.

Gina screamed and began backing out of the room. The grim-faced criminal started forward, the eery light now on his face. Gina fell over a chair, and at that moment she heard the front door burst open and footsteps charge toward her.

Startled, Blackchurch looked up. Then with a snarl he turned and dashed out the kitchen door and was gone.

Detective Lombard appeared a split second later, his blast gun out and his eyes scanning the room. Gina was caught between terror and surprise as she realized she'd never seen her father in his role as a trained fighter, weapon out and ready.

"What happened?" he said in a tight voice.

"I—I saw," she stammered. "It was him! He was here!"

Her father's eyes scanned the room again. "Who?"

"Blackchurch!" she sputtered. "He was right here in this room!"

The clenched look on her father's face relaxed into mild confusion. He holstered his weapon and helped her to her feet. "Honey, Blackchurch's been gone for two months. He vanished in a fireball about 10 million miles out into space."

Gina remembered the techie's words: *They never found his body.* "Maybe he escaped. He was here, Dad. I saw him right here."

"Well, I'm sure you saw somebody," her father said, "and that means someone was in our house."

Faster than she could say "But, Dad—" Detective Lombard was on the phone. Half an hour later, two uniformed officers were stationed in front of the house and two more in the back. Gina argued that the man was Blackchurch until she was too exhausted to argue anymore. She'd been up all night, let alone nearly attacked by a notorious criminal—who was supposed to be dead but really wasn't. The stress had drained all her energy, and her father practically carried her to bed.

"But, Dad—" she tried again.

"Just close your eyes, Gina," her dad said. "You're perfectly safe now. There are police officers everywhere. And I'll come check on you in a bit."

Gina did close her eyes, and instantly she fell asleep. But despite her exhaustion, her sleep was fitful and full of dreams.

She kept seeing Dr. Ruger's holographic face. He was trying to tell her something, but the holophone was broken and no sound came through. Then to her surprise, Dr. Ruger's hand reached right out of the hologram—which was impossible—and tugged at her arm. Instantly she could hear him speak. *"Gina, Gina!"*

"Gina . . . Gina . . ." she heard through her sleep. Someone actually was tugging at her arm and speaking to her. She blinked to clear the sleep from her eyes, figuring it was her father. She opened her eyes.

Blackchurch was standing over her.

This time he wasn't glaring. He was grinning an evil grin that lit his face with a nasty glow. "You done me a big favor, bringin' me here," he said in a gravelly voice. "So I'm gonna get you last of all. But I'll start with your dad."

Then he seemed to swirl away. Gina cried out, and her father burst into the room, followed by two police officers.

Blackchurch was gone.

"Dad! Dad!" she yelled, sobbing as she told him what had happened.

Detective Lombad's disbelief was obvious. "No one came in or out of this house, Gina," he said. "You must have been dreaming."

"It wasn't a dream," she insisted. "He's alive and he's here."

"Blackchurch is dead!" her father said, raising his voice. "I chased that sorry excuse for a human being out into space and I saw his ship explode."

Gina shook her head. "Well, maybe he had an escape pod

or maybe he never even was onboard, but I saw him right where you're standing."

Still her father wouldn't believe her. Just how Blackchurch had slipped out so quickly, Gina couldn't answer. Surrendering for the moment, she agreed to try to sleep some more. The police officers would investigate the grounds around the house.

Maybe it was a dream, she thought as she stared at the ceiling.

But that didn't explain the first encounter.

So if Blackchurch really was alive, and if he did want some sort of revenge on Gina's dad, why had he waited all this time? What had triggered his sudden appearance?

The answer was obvious. The mood ring. Blackchurch had been a brilliant criminal, capable of complicated computer crime. Perhaps he'd hacked into the WETworks database and planted a bug that would alert him if anyone looked up his records. Maybe that was his way of alerting himself that he was suspected of still being alive.

Mulling over that mystery, Gina recalled another. Dr. Ruger had warned her she was in danger. And now she was. How had he known?

There was only one way to find out.

Gina got up and stretched, then walked casually out of her bedroom, across the living room, and into the kitchen. "Glass of water," she said to her dad, who was talking with one of the uniformed officers.

In the kitchen, she filled a glass of water, then picked up her backpack, which she'd dropped during Blackchurch's first assault. Nonchalantly she carried the water and the backpack back to her room and shut the door. As soon as she was out of sight, she yanked the holophone and mood ring out of the pack and made sure the connections were still secure. Then she powered up both devices and called Dr. Ruger.

Just as before there was a delay, but eventually Dr. Ruger's head appeared. His worried expression deepened the wrinkles on his nearly 60-year-old forehead.

"I'm still alive," she said to him.

"Evidently," the scientist said. "But still in great, great danger!"

"How do you know?"

Ruger laughed. "I know a great many things, more things than I thought I would ever know. But that is a story for another time. Right now, I must tell you that what you have done is enormously harmful. It could be the end of everything!"

"What do you mean?" Gina asked. "What's going on?"

"What do you think is going on!" Ruger snorted. "You think Blackchurch is alone? He plans to bring more of his kind in on this. If you're not careful, you'll be overwhelmed by hundreds, maybe thousands, just like Blackchurch."

Hundreds? Thousands? "Is he planning some sort of attack? Does he want to overthrow the government?"

"The government!" Ruger snorted. "The world! The universe! And you must stop him."

"How?" Gina asked.

"Fortunately, the answer is simple. You must—zzzzzz!" the hologram crackled and snapped. It faded out, then came back.

"What's wrong with this thing?" Gina said.

"He is interfering with the signal somehow. He can do that, you know. He's far more powerful than you—zzzzzzz!" The image crackled again, and this time when it faded out, it did not return.

"Sorry, girlie. Can't allow that."

Blackchurch was in her room again.

This time Gina didn't cry out. She stared at him, getting a good look. It was Blackchurch indeed. The same hard, square face, the same look of pure evil.

"Whatever you're up to, my dad will stop you!" Gina threatened.

Blackchurch only laughed. "What's he gonna do, kill me? I don't think so. Not now that I got this whole thing figured out. No one can stop me, and once I have that little machine you got there, I'm takin' over the world!"

He stepped forward, but Gina moved faster. She bolted for the door and ran straight into the living room, practially slamming into her father.

"What the—?" the detective said.

"He's here again! Blackchurch!" she yelled.

"Gina," her father groaned.

"No, honest, Dad!" she said. "And I can prove it! Professor Ruger believes me. He knows what's going on. I just talked to him!"

Detective Lombard blinked. "You just talked to him?"

"Yeah."

"To Dr. Ruger, the man who invented the mood ring?"

"Yeah!"

Her father frowned and looked at the police officer standing across the room. Then he said, "Gina, Dr. Ruger was murdered three days ago."

His words hit Gina like a star cruiser at light speed. The breath left her body, and the hairs stood up on the back of her neck. "He . . . he was murdered?" she said. "Well, then, Blackchurch must have done it. Because he knows something . . ."

"Three days ago, Gina," her father said gently. "In fact, it was his murder I was investigating last night. That's the crime scene you visited. Someone killed him. And we've already got a lead on the killer. He's confessed to killing Ruger."

"But . . . but it can't be," she said. "I just talked to the doctor."

"You couldn't have," he explained. Then he added gently, "Gina, I think maybe you're not feeling well."

"And you ain't gonna be feeling too well soon enough, Detective."

Everyone turned in the direction of the unannounced voice. There stood the man Detective Lombard had chased all the way to the end of his life.

Detective Lombard's face drained of all color. "Impossible."

"Yeah, I know," Blackchurch agreed. "But here I am anyway."

Without another word, Detective Lombard drew his weapon and fired. A powerful energy beam streaked across the short space between them but passed harmlessly through Blackchurch, smashing into the wall behind him.

Blackchurch laughed and stormed forward.

Bravely the police officer charged out to meet him. He tried to tackle Blackchurch, but his hands sank right through him, without taking hold. Blackchurch, however, had no such difficulty. His hand gripped the officer's throat and squeezed until the man fell unconscious.

Detective Lombard fired again. Just as before, the energy bolt passed harmlessly through Blackchurch's body, and by this time the evil doer was on them. He slapped the weapon from Lombard's hand, then grabbed him by the shirt collar and punched him, sending him halfway across the room. Without a pause, he turned to Gina. But instead of grabbing her, he snatched the mood ring and the holophone from her hands.

"First things first," he said. "Then I can take care of you two whenever I want."

Blackchurch carried the mood ring to the middle of the room and began to punch in codes. He seemed totally unconcerned about Gina or her father. "Now, let's see here," he said to himself. "Yeah, this thing can access the entire WETworks database and its information on criminals. Ha! Might as well start at the top."

Gina hurried over to her father, who was just recovering from Blackchurch's blow. "Dad, are you—?"

"This can't be happening," her father said. "He should be dead. No one can survive two laser blasts like that."

"They didn't seem to touch him," she said. "It's like he isn't really there."

"Oh, he's there all right," her father said, rubbing his jaw. "Trust me. I'm telling you, that man died two months ago! He was vaporized!"

And Gina had talked to another dead man. Twice. It didn't make sense.

At least, not until Gina glanced up and saw the holographic image that Blackchurch had somehow managed to summon through the mood ring. The figure was as tall and grim as Blackchurch, but he was missing an eye. Standing in the glow of the mood ring, he snarled at the two observers.

"Who's that?" Gina asked.

Her father was nearly speechless. "That's . . . that's Mike Stone. He used to be part of Blackchurch's gang. But he was . . . he was killed in a gunfight with police years ago."

Another dead man. Another . . .

And, like solving the pieces of her other puzzles, Gina solved this one.

They were ghosts. She had been talking to ghosts.

Somehow the alterations she'd made to the mood ring had boosted the signal way beyond her intentions. Instead of just reading energy signatures that were older, the mood ring reached back through the energy trail and found the original person.

Even if he or she were dead.

The device was bringing back the dead. Suddenly, Dr. Ruger's words made sense: *Right now, I must tell you that what you have done is enormously harmful.*

Gina had opened a door to the next world.

Mike Stone started to step into the room.

But Gina knew what to do. She snatched up the gun and handed it to her father. "Dad, shoot!"

Her father held up the gun as if it were a hunk of useless metal. "It won't hurt them."

"Not them!" she yelled. "The mood ring!"

Her father shrugged and took aim. "No!" the two ghosts yelled. Blackchurch charged forward while his accomplice leaped protectively in front of the device. The energy bolt passed through both of them easily and struck the mood ring. The device exploded in a shower of sparks.

"NO!" Blackchurch bellowed. He reached out to throttle Detective Lombard, but even as his hands got around the policeman's throat, they started to fade away. In seconds, both ghosts had vanished, leaving Gina and her father exhausted.

"That," her father said at last, "will take some explaining."

"I . . . I was just trying to fix the mood ring," Gina explained. "I was trying to boost its signal."

"I'll say," her father said, shaking his head in utter bewilderment. "You boosted it all the way to the world beyond."

"And . . . and I talked to Dr. Ruger," she said, feeling both elation and fear. "I talked to a ghost."

"You always were ahead of your time," her father said. "I hope he was nice."

"He was," Gina said. "I wonder what it's like in the next world."

Her father laughed and slowly stood up. "Well, that's one mystery even you won't be eager to figure out!"

High Society

None of this would have happened if I hadn't dropped the egg off the city's edge, Quil thought.

He was standing knee-deep in filthy water. Bloodflies buzzed around his ears and swarmed in clouds around his feathered head. Flexing his neck muscles, he raised his feather crest with a *snap,* driving the flies away. But only for a second—they were back again soon enough.

At that moment he wished feathers covered his entire body, like a bird. As a Makau, Quil had only a small crown of feathers atop his head. Plus, his little orange and purple crest wasn't that impressive. Not like his father's bright crown of red, yellow, and blue.

Father, Quil thought, dragging one leg forward through the muck with a *shlopping* sound. *He's going to have me plucked when he finds out about this.*

Quil had to admit he'd brought everything on himself.

It certainly had been an unusual day, starting with his visit to his father's office . . .

———

"I didn't know we had a meeting scheduled today," Quil's father said.

Quil smoothed back his ruffled head feathers and tried to relax. "Um, we didn't, Father," he said timidly. "But I was hoping I could speak with you."

Quil's father stood up and walked around from behind his desk. He wore a coat of bright colors—the reds, blues, and yellows favored by most Makau businessmen. Makau males prided themselves on their sense of style, and Quil's father was no exception.

"Well, it's a bit out of the ordinary," his father said. He picked up a palm-sized computer off his desk and punched in a command. "Didn't we just have a father-son talk the other day? We don't have another one scheduled until next week."

"I know, sir," Quil said. He waited for his father to ask him to sit down, but the offer never came. Quil's feather crest started to rise a bit in irritation. He realized he was breaking with custom by talking to his father without an appointment, but couldn't his dad at least offer him a seat?

Finally he said, "But, um, well . . . I've been having trouble in school."

"Trouble in school," his father repeated. He punched in more commands on his hand computer. "Really? Nothing's showing up on the latest report from your teacher."

"It's not my grades, Father," Quil said. "It's . . ."

He stopped. He'd spent the whole trip down here on the hoverbus planning what to say. But now that he was standing in front of his father, he couldn't bring himself to say the words he'd been practicing: *Father, I feel lost. I'm growing up too fast and I feel awkward and clumsy and stupid, and I need advice from you.*

That's what he'd wanted to say. But now he just couldn't. He looked around for something, anything to talk about instead.

On his father's desk was the holographic picture of a large egg. The egg, when it hatched, was going to be his new brother or sister. "Um, can you tell me more about my new sibling?" he said lamely.

His father's crest feathers rose up for a minute, then settled back down as he sighed, "Quil, I'm afraid I don't have time for this. And, if you'll check your scheduler, you'll see that you and I are set to talk about family matters in less than a month. Until then, I'm afraid you'll have to let me do my work. Good day, son."

His father shooed him out of the office.

Quil was almost relieved. It had been a mistake coming down here.

Shoulders drooping, he left the office building and stepped onto the city streets. Pulling his jacket tight around his body, he hugged his arms to his sides. This time of year, the winds were cold. Quil had always heard that Chirripa's surface was warmer than its skies, but he had no way of knowing if that were true. He had never been to the planet's surface.

The city where he lived hovered in the air about a half mile above land. Held aloft by huge antigravity generators, it drifted over the green landscape of Chirripa like an island in the sky.

Suspended in the heavens, Quil's home city of Aerie was a marvel of technology. Sixty miles wide and twenty across, it held nearly two million Makau, a spaceport, a dozen parks, a sports stadium, office buildings, and thousands of nests where Makau families lived. Hundreds of hoverbarges traveled to and from Aerie each day, trafficking between that city and the other Makau cities floating above the surface of the planet.

But Makau technology did not stop with antigravity machinery. Nearly every aspect of Makau life was automated: scheduled and assigned, organized and tracked by the tiny palm-top computers most Makaus owned. The Makau even programmed the way they raised their children.

Quil reached his own building and looked up. He and his family lived in a high-rise. To the Makau way of thinking, the higher up you lived, the more important you were, and Quil's family lived in the topmost nest.

A weight settled on Quil's shoulders as he stepped onto the floater that would carry him up to the top floor. Automatically sensors recognized him and started the floater toward his home. On the way he passed the balconies of dozens of other nests. Even the poorest Makaus managed to have balconies allowing them to feel the open air. That was one thing no Makau could do without.

The floater stopped at Quil's nest and he stepped off. He looked around at the elegant furnishings in his home. His father was a successful trader in antiques. His parents provided him with the best of everything. And they had purchased the most expensive parenting computer programs available to make sure they raised him properly.

But Quil wasn't happy.

He sat down in the living room and looked around. On a wall screen he saw blinking lights that showed his own daily schedule along with the schedules of both his parents.

But something's missing, Quil brooded.

He got up and wandered around. His footsteps took him to the heart of the nest: the nursery. There, under warm lights in a bed of soft cloth, sat the egg. It was the same egg he'd seen in the holograph on his father's desk. Round and brown, it had little white speckles all over it.

"I feel about as dumb as you look," Quil said out loud. "I don't know what I was thinking, going to see father without an appointment. He's about as straitlaced as a Makau can get."

Quil sat down next to the egg. Centuries ago, Makau females laid eggs, and Makau males sat on them to keep them warm until they hatched. Now once a female laid them, eggs were put under special lights that kept them healthy. Special music and recordings of their parents' voices were played to comfort and reassure the hatchlings-to-be inside. Then the parents went off to work.

"Boy, are you in for it," he said out loud to the egg. "You know, they can tell you the exact minute you'll hatch. They can even tell you what you're going to be when you grow up." He shook his head and puffed up his crest feathers angrily. "It's like, what's the point of going through it if your whole life's already planned out?"

Quil leaned forward and picked up the egg. He'd never touched it before. He wasn't allowed. In fact, almost no one touched the egg at all, except once every week or so when his mother rotated it in its nest.

Quil hugged the egg close, trying to spark some warm and tender feelings inside himself. After all, it was going to be his brother or sister someday.

But all he felt was empty. Not knowing what else to do, he carried the egg to the balcony.

Out on the ledge he held the egg up high and said, "Some view, huh?"

The view was spectacular. Not only was his family's nest one of the highest in the city, it was also right on the city's edge. That meant they had an unobstructed view of the planet below. Instead of the fabricated streets and buildings of Aerie, they looked out over the wide rivers and steamy jungles where the Makau had lived centuries ago.

"Now that's something to look forward to," Quil said to the egg. "I bet you'll like this as much as I do. You know, when I'm feeling kind of sad and molty, I come out here and just look at the scenery. It makes me feel better. I don't know why."

Quil leaned forward, holding the egg tight. "You know, they say there are still Makau living down on the surface. I mean, not real Makau, like us. More like savages. Makau who didn't want to migrate to the cities. They say they don't even look like us anymore. But they're down there."

Quil looked down, wishing he could see past the tangle of green trees far below him.

At that moment, something inside the egg moved. The egg trembled, and there was a sound like a peck from inside the shell. Quil was so startled, he loosened his grip.

And the next thing he knew, the egg was falling.

—

Quil could still feel the terror of that moment when he watched the egg fall. As the egg dropped through the air, his heart had dropped into his stomach, opening up a huge pit of fear.

Soon the egg had vanished into a green canopy of trees.

Quil could at least be certain the egg hadn't broken. That's because Makau eggs weren't fragile like bird eggs. Instead their shells were tough as leather. And the hatchlings inside were further protected by layers of jellylike fluid. That's how, in the early days before technology, Makaus had been able to survive on a planet as harsh as Chirripa. None of the predators on the planet could ever eat their eggs.

Still wading through the murky waters of the swamp, Quil looked around nervously. *But they can eat full-grown Makau,* he thought grimly.

Once he'd recovered from the shock of dropping the egg, Quil knew exactly what he had to do: go find it.

It didn't matter that it was against the law to go down to the planet's surface. The law couldn't punish him any worse than his father once he discovered what Quil had done.

Getting to the surface had been remarkably easy. Aerie was filled with hovercabs that took residents wherever they wanted to go. Quil had simply hailed one and gotten inside. "Planet surface," he had said to the computerized pilot. After double- and triple-checking the command, the hovercab had obeyed. It wasn't programmed to deny that request, because no one, absolutely no one, was insane enough to travel to the planet's surface.

Now I know why, Quil thought. He'd grown up hearing about the dangers of Chirripa's surface: the meerhawks that liked to eat young Makau, the razorfish that swam in large schools through the shallow water and could tear the skin off your bones in seconds. But most of all, he'd heard about the left-behinds. The Saurans.

Saurans were essentially the same species as the Makau. In appearance, anyway, they were alike, with two arms and two legs and similar faces. But instead of a feathered crest on their head, they had a hard leather ridge.

As a child, Quil had heard the old denmother's tale about the Saurans. He could still remember it now: *Now you be a good boy, Quil. Do you know what happens to bad little boys? They get careless and fall off the edge of the city. That's what happened to the Saurans, you know. They were bad little boys and girls who fell off the edge of the city and lost their feathers on the way down.*

In science class, Quil had learned the real story. At some point long ago, Makaus had evolved from Saurans, growing crests on their heads and taking an interest in flight. That's when they had built the hovering cities. But the Saurans refused to evolve, remaining savage and primitive, so the Makau had to force them out of the cities and back to the planet's surface.

And that's a fate worse than death, Quil thought. He slapped at a fly that was trying to sting his neck.

He was sure he'd guided the hovercab to the right spot. Of course, he couldn't be certain exactly where the egg had landed, but it had to be somewhere in the area.

Thick, gnarled trees stretched out in every direction. Their leafy branches completely blocked out the sky in places. A shallow pool of water covered the planet's surface, except for mounds of wet earth that managed to poke up from the dark water. Tufts of bristly grass grew on the mounds.

Quil found one of these tiny islands and stopped to rest. Nearby, on another patch of ground, he spotted a little green reptile squatting in the grass. It had a huge round head, tiny front legs, and back legs so long that even bent they were twice the length of the rest of its body. Swelling up its throat, the little reptile let out a loud *blurp!*

"What, are you telling me I'd better keep looking?" Quil said irritably. "Well, you're probably right." He stood up and stepped down into the slimy water.

Startled by his movement, the little creature *blurped* again and dived into the water with a splash.

"Yeah, well I didn't want to spend any more time with you either," Quil said. He stomped through the water for a few more steps when he heard another splash.

Turning, he saw the creature thrashing in the water. The creature let out a panicked *blurp!* In the midst of the thrashing water, Quil saw other little bodies—wriggling bodies with red and gold scales, pointed purple fins, and sharp, spiny teeth.

Razorfish!

Quil started to sprint back toward the tiny island, but the deadly fish were between him and safety. He looked up, hoping to climb a tree, but realized the branches were too high. Panicked, he turned and ran the other way.

He shouldn't have.

Attracted by the splashing water, the razorfish turned away from the little reptile and started toward larger prey. There were so many of them and they moved so quickly, they swelled the water like a bulge in a carpet.

Looking back over his shoulder, Quil noticed the swell racing toward him. Terrified, he kept running, wincing in anticipation of thousands of razor-sharp teeth biting his legs. Risking a glance over his shoulder, he saw the swell of swarming fish nearly at his heels.

Just as he felt the sting of the first bite, Quil was aware of something snagging onto the back of his shirt. Before he knew it, he was lifted out of the water. He hung there, suspended in midair. Beneath him the razorfish swarmed, some leaping out of the water and snapping at him. He curled his feet up under his body to avoid them. Their frenzied splashing continued a few more seconds and then, realizing they'd missed their meal, the school swam away.

"Um, you could help me here," came a voice from above.

Startled, Quil looked up and saw that he hadn't gotten snagged on something but on someone. Lying across a thick branch above him was a girl. She was holding onto the collar of his jacket with one hand and gripping the tree limb with the other. Both arms were trembling with the effort.

"Should I pull myself up?" he asked.

"Too late," she said. Her strength gave out and she dropped him. Quil landed on the seat of his pants in the water. Terrified, he jumped to his feet and scrambled for the nearest mound and sat there, panting in exhaustion.

Calmly the girl dropped from the tree branch. She landed on her feet, making almost no splash in the water, and glided over to him.

"Don't worry," she said. "That's the thing about razorfish. They're vicious, but they don't stay in one place for long."

Quil looked at the girl who saved his life. She was a little shorter than he was, and he guessed that she was about his age. She wore trousers that reached just below her knees—which kept them mostly out of the water—and a baggy pullover shirt. She also carried a satchel across her back. Her face was dirty, but when she saw him looking at her she smiled, and even through the muck he could see she was pretty. Finally, Quil's eyes came to rest on the top of her head. He couldn't disguise his horror when he realized she had no feathered crest. Her head was topped by a thin leathery ridge.

"Y-you're a Sauran," he gasped.

She shrugged. "You say it like it's an insult."

He swallowed, not sure whether to be more afraid of her than of the razorfish. "I . . . I'm sorry. It's just that I've never seen one of you before."

"That's okay," she said with another smile. "We call you people featherheads. So I guess we're even. My name is Dinah."

She held out her hand. Quil hesitated but finally shook it. Her skin felt as warm as his own—though more calloused.

"Um, thanks," he said at last. "I'm Quil. I guess you saved my life."

She nodded. "You've got to watch out for razorfish. They can sneak up on you. Always good to have a tree nearby." She plopped down on the ground next to him. "So, what brings you down here? We don't see many of you folk. Once in a while a ship flies through, but never with kids like you on it."

He looked up at the sky. Through a break in the trees, he could see Aerie floating in the distance. It was miles off by now.

"I . . . I dropped something," he said. "And I have to get it back or I'm gonna get plucked."

She laughed and ruffled the feathers on his head. "Get plucked. That's funny!"

Quil stiffened when she touched him. No one had ever touched him that playfully before. Not his parents, not his friends. Makaus just didn't do that.

Dinah jumped to her feet. "Well, Quil, you're not gonna be able to find anything here on your own. Not unless what you want to find is razorfish. Lemme take you back to my village and see if we can be of any help."

She started off through the water.

With a shrug, Quil followed.

Dinah led him through the swamp. At first her course seemed to zigzag without purpose, but after a while Quil realized she was tracking the shallowest parts of the water. Eventually her course led them up onto dry land. There she pulled off the wet shoes she wore—which he realized were made of waterproof rubber—and slipped on dry shoes, which she'd carried in her satchel.

"Ah, nothing like dry feet!" she said in a bubbly voice and started off again.

As Dinah led him along a crooked path through a forest of crooked trees, Quil studied her. Other than her lack of feathers, she was very much like the girls he knew from school. Except that she was friendlier and more relaxed than any Makau he'd ever met in his life.

But still, she was filthy by Makau standards. And she lived in this . . . this jungle. "How do you live here?" he asked as they walked.

She looked at him as if the question made no sense. She pointed to the distant city in the sky. "How do you live up there?"

"Well, it's easy," he started to say. "We just . . ." Then he stopped. How did you describe to someone how you lived?

I eat. I go to school. I do my homework. Sometimes I talk with my friends. That was one way he could have put it.

I have to make appointments to see my parents. Every moment of my life is scheduled by computers. That was another way.

He decided not to answer her.

Before long, sounds met them from the path ahead: the chatter of voices, the clang and bang of metal. As the sounds grew louder, the path opened up and flowed into a wide village. The little town was made up of one-story houses scattered around a clearing. Two or three main streets wound their way lazily in and among the houses. A number of small Saurans played at chasing one another between the buildings or tossing little rubber balls against the walls.

The banging came from some sort of workshop, where a tall male Sauran stood over a fire pit. He was holding a piece of metal into the fire, then taking it out, laying it on a flat iron table, and banging it into a new shape with a hammer.

"That's my dad," Dinah said. "Let's see if he can help."

"Wait!" Quil said. "Don't you need an appointment?"

"A what?" Dinah asked as she trotted over to her father.

He had stopped his work by now, noticing the newcomer in the village. The Sauran eyed Quil closely, studying his brightly feathered crest. It wasn't an unfriendly look. In fact, it was friendlier than any look Quil had gotten at home.

"Hi, Dad!" Dinah said. "Look who I found in the swamp. He's from up there!"

Before saying anything, the Sauran leaned over and grabbed Dinah. For a split second, Quil thought he was angry at being interrupted and was attacking the girl. But then he realized her father was gathering her into a warm embrace.

Could this really be her *father*?

Only after hugging her did the Sauran turn toward Quil.

"So I see," he said. He wiped his hands on his apron and then held one out to Quil. "Duk's my name. Glad to meet you, young fellow."

"Th-thank you, sir," Quil said. "I'm Quil."

"He needs help finding something," Dinah explained.

"Um, yes," Quil said. He was feeling uncomfortable, like a visitor to an alien planet. "I . . . I dropped something off the edge of the city. It fell somewhere around here."

"Dropped something, eh?" Duk asked. What sort of something?"

Quil swallowed his embarrassment. "An egg."

"An egg!" Duk said. "Well, that is worth looking for, isn't it?"

"Maybe even worth getting eaten for," Dinah said. "Quil here was about to be razorfish snacks when I found him."

Duk grunted. "Got to watch out for razorfish, that's for sure. Glad you're all right, son!" The Sauran ruffled Quil's head feathers.

The touch startled him, just like before. But it also made him tingle all over. He decided he liked it.

"Can you . . . can you help me find the egg?" he asked.

Duk laughed. "As a matter of fact, I think I can. Come this way." He started walking toward the center of the village.

Quil hesitated. "But I think it's back there." He pointed toward the swamp.

Duk ignored him and kept walking, so Quil had no choice but to follow. The Sauran led him to a round house in the middle of the town. Around it, dozens of children played games of tag and hide-and-seek. All of them stopped when they saw Quil, but like Duk, the looks they gave him were friendly.

Duk led Quil and Dinah into the building, which consisted of one big room. In the center a few dozen Sauran children gathered around a single Sauran female, who was telling them a story.

As he got closer, Quil could see that the female was holding something in her hand.

"My egg!" he said.

"Sh," Duk whispered. "Story time."

The female Sauran was saying, ". . . and as the days passed, more and more people grew feathers on their heads, as beautiful as crowns. They were very beautiful, and they knew that they were beautiful. This made them very proud."

Quil found himself charmed by her voice. She spoke with caring and love, her eyes moving from one Sauran child to another as if talking to just him or her. The Makau boy found himself remembering something vaguely, something from his hatchling years. He remembered his mother cooing over him, looking at him the way this Sauran woman looked at all these grown children. She even looked the same way at the egg in her arms, rocking it as she spoke.

"One day, the feathered ones said, 'We are too beautiful to live down here on the ground. We belong in the skies.' So they built cities in the clouds. They asked the Saurans to join them, but the Saurans stayed behind. 'We like to have our feet on the ground,' the Saurans said. 'That way it's easier to hug our children!' " And she reached forward to the closest child and gave it a surprise squeeze. The child squawked with laughter, and the laughter spread.

"All right, children," said the female. "Story time is over. Play outside while the sun shines!"

All the children rose and scampered out, hardly noticing Quil among them. The female noticed, though, and walked over to where he stood with Duk and Dinah.

"Hi, Mama!" Dinah said. "Look who I met today."

"I'm Quil, ma'am," Quil said, finally remembering his manners.

"Nice to meet you, young man," she replied. She hesitated a moment, hugging the egg a little closer to her body. Then she said, "This must be yours."

"Yes, ma'am," he said.

She held it a moment longer. This confused Quil. After all, it wasn't hers. How could she have grown so attached to it so quickly? Finally, she said, "It's all right in there. The fall didn't hurt it one bit. That little hatchling's going to be just fine." Then, with some effort, she gave it over to him.

"Thanks, ma'm," he said.

Duk smiled and put a hand on the female's shoulder. "You'll have to forgive my wife, son. We tend to cling to our young ones here. We only just found your egg. Nearly plopped down into the middle of my forge, if you want to know. But, well, you get a mother to hold a young one and you know what happens."

Quil blinked. *No, I don't know,* he thought. *At least, I didn't until now.*

"Um, ma'am," he asked. "Do you mind if I ask a question? Why were you holding the egg like that? I mean, it's just an egg right now."

"Well, right now," she said. "But there's a child in there somewhere. And we teach our children that we love them from the get-go."

"Well, thanks," he said. "I should be getting back before I get into trouble."

"Before he gets plucked!" Dinah laughed. "Come on, I'll take you back to where your hovercab is."

"Have a safe trip, Quil!" Duk said. "Keep your feet dry!"

"And take care of that little hatchling. It's a special one!" his wife called.

With Dinah's guidance, the trip back to the hovercab was uneventful. The cab was waiting where Quil had told it to wait. As he climbed in, he turned to Dinah. "That story your mother was telling. What was it?"

"Oh, that." Dinah shrugged. "Just a game that moms play. It's an excuse to give their kids a hug."

"We tell the same story up on Aerie," he said, thinking of the old hen's tale he'd been told as a hatchling. "Only it's totally different."

Dinah shrugged again. "Well, I guess your people have their way and my people have mine."

"Fair enough," he said. "One more question?"

"Sure."

"Your mother said she wanted her children to learn early on that she loved them. How did she . . . how did you learn that?"

Dinah thought a minute. "I guess I always knew. Or maybe she just kept showing me until I got it." She started down the path. "Good-bye!"

"Bye," he said, getting into the cab.

—

A few minutes later, the hovercab had caught up to the city. It flew Quil straight home. He jumped out and ignored the stares of passersby who gawked at his muddy clothes. Then he hopped onboard the floater and let it zip him up to the top floor. Hurrying inside, he carried the egg to its nest under the warm lights.

He'd done it. He'd gotten the egg back. He wasn't going to get plucked.

But just as he was about to put the egg down, he hesitated. He remembered the way the Sauran had held it, cradled in her arms. Like she . . . like she *loved* it.

Instead of putting the egg down, he held it for a while, rocking it gently. He didn't have any stories to tell. He had no words to say. So he just hummed softly as he rocked it, back and forth.

That's how his parents found him when they came home from work.

"Quil, what are you doing?" his father said. "There's no egg rotation scheduled for tonight."

"I know, Father," he said. "I'm just . . ." he gathered himself, finding the courage to say what he couldn't earlier that day. "I'm just showing it that I love it."

He didn't know how long it would take for the older Makau to understand. But someday he would, if Quil tried hard enough.

"You know, son," his father said. "That egg really can't understand anything yet. Not until it's a hatchling."

Quil nodded, but he was looking at his father, not the egg, when he said, "I know, but I'll just keep doing it until he understands."

Accidents Happen

The star freighter *Never Better* landed gently on the flight strip of the main spaceport on Calabi-Yau. Inside, Milo Forecastle leaned back in his seat and put his feet up on the control panels. He yawned. The flight had been boring, the descent had been boring—now the landing was boring. His father, Dr. Hal Forecastle, was an old-time star pilot who did everything by the book.

Now if Milo had been old enough to get a pilot's license, things would have been different.

"Okay, sport," his father said, turning toward him with a serious expression. "You remember the deal?"

"Yeah, Dad," Milo groaned. *Do we have to go through this again?* "I'm not supposed to get involved in local affairs," he droned.

"Check," his dad said, frowning. "I know what you're thinking, and yes, we *do* have to go over it again. Calabi-Yau is on friendly terms with Earth and the other planets in the Trade

Alliance, but it's not a member. That means we've got to stick to a hands-off policy. I'm just here to do my job, and that's all."

Dr. Forecastle worked as an energineer. He specialized in machinery and technology that produced energy, like power plants. The Calabi were experiencing some sort of energy crisis, and they'd asked the Trade Alliance to send someone to help.

"Help" wasn't as simple as it sounded. Members of the Trade Alliance acted under strict rules. One of the most important was the Law of Preservation. Hal and Milo could only pitch in to solve a particular problem. They were absolutely forbidden from interfering with the natives' way of life.

Unfortunately, Milo thought, *dad isn't forbidden from interfering in* my *life.*

"I really don't want to be here." Meaning to say this under his breath, Milo in fact had spoken loudly enough to be heard.

His dad rubbed his temples as if trying to get rid of a headache. "I know, son. You'd rather be back home air-surfing on the underside of hovercars or doing some other daredevil stunt."

"Hey, the vid networks pay a lot of money for stunts like that. If I get good enough, I could make it as a video star—"

"That's playworld, Milo," his father said. "But this is the real galaxy. You have to live in it sooner or later. You're almost 14 years old, and it's . . ."

". . . time I started thinking about my future," Milo said the words along with his dad. He'd heard them plenty of times before.

"When I was your age I'd already started taking advanced energineering classes." The elder Forecastle tried to soften his voice. "Milo, you have a real talent for energy engineering. You could be a lot better than I am. But you don't apply yourself."

"I do apply myself, Dad," he protested. "Just not to the things you want me to."

The ship touched down with a jolt, interrupting their conversation. *Just as well,* thought Milo, *since once again they were headed for an argument.*

As the hatch opened, Milo and his father stepped out into bright sunlight and a sky that was more purple than blue.

At the edge of the flight strip a tall Calabi male and a small Calabi female waited.

This was Milo's first look at Calabi natives, and immediately he wondered if all the males were this tall and all the females this pretty. From a distance, the Calabis looked very much like humans, except their skin was pale blue. But as he got closer, Milo saw that a soft layer of fur covered their bodies. Their faces were round, their noses like buttons.

He guessed that the female was about 14 or 15, though with alien species, age was often hard to tell.

The Calabi male stepped forward. "Dr. Forecastle, I am Sensen Kaleef Dharma, Chief Operator of the Geothermal Tap. Welcome."

He dipped his head in an odd sort of bow that was apparently a Calabi form of greeting. It was only then that Milo saw the Calabi's long, graceful tail hovering in the air behind him. Calabis, Milo realized, looked very much like cats.

Sensen Dharma held out his hand and Milo's dad shook it. "Thank you, sir," Dr. Forecastle said. "This is my son, Milo. I hope you don't mind. I called ahead to say that he'd be coming along. He'll make a fine energineer himself some day."

Sensen Dharma smiled. "He is most welcome. In fact, this is my daughter, Dani. She has a future as a diplomat, and I thought she might be able to act as your son's guide on our planet."

"Hi," Milo said to the female Calabi.

"Greetings," Dani replied. Then she leaned forward and kissed Milo full on the lips, her blue fur tickling his nose. He jumped back, startled.

"Oh," Dani considered. Her fur quivered and changed from a pale blue to a light pink color. Then she grabbed her tail, hiding behind it like a veil. "Wasn't that the right way to greet someone from Earth?"

Sensen Dharma put a hand on his daughter's shoulder. "I believe that sort of greeting is reserved for when humans know each other better."

"At least a little better," Milo said. His lips burned where the girl had kissed him.

"I'm sorry," she apologized.

"No harm done," he said.

Sensen Dharma quickly overcame the awkward moment with a remark. "We have taken the liberty of assigning rooms for you at a local mirkirrado. I believe you call such a place a hotel. It is located just outside the spaceport so we can walk if you like. I thought you might enjoy seeing a bit of our city."

"Excellent," Hal Forecastle said.

Milo and his father followed the Calabi to a small ground vehicle that drove them to the main terminal. There, Dr. Forecastle officially registered his ship with the authorities. Then they left the terminal and walked out onto the streets of the city.

Like any major city in the galaxy, it was filled with sights and sounds and smells. Ground vehicles rumbled along on two or three or four wheels. Flying craft floated overhead. Calabis hurried by on foot. The Calabi moved gracefully, like dancers.

Milo glanced around. The buildings looked pretty much like buildings on most planets, although the Calabi didn't seem to like sharp edges. Most of the buildings had curves instead of corners, and their tops ended in domes rather than in flat or sloped roofs. The taller buildings seemed to sway with the same grace as the Calabi themselves.

"There's the mirkirrado," Dani said.

She pointed across the street at a building painted white with green trim. "Green is the color of welcome, and white is for rest," she explained.

Suddenly a deafening screech filled the air and a great gust of wind rose up, nearly blowing them off their feet. Milo staggered back. Just then, something huge and hot and yellow streaked past him. The force of its passing knocked him off his feet, while its intense brightness made him shut his eyes. There was a sound like a rocket thruster firing, and a moment later an explosion shook the air.

Milo opened his eyes and got to his feet. The air, now filled with dust, made him cough. As the dust cleared he looked around. His father, Sensen Dharma, and Dani were still there. Everything, in fact, seemed normal.

Except that the mirkirrado had vanished. All that remained was a pile of rubble and a cloud of dust settling over it.

"Milo, are you okay?" his father asked.

"Y-yeah, I guess," he said. "What was that?"

They both looked at Dani and Sensen Dharma. To Milo's surprise, the Calabi seemed totally unfazed by what had happened. Dani simply flicked dust off her tail and smoothed a wrinkle in her blouse, while her father brushed dust from his neat brown uniform.

"Well," Sensen Dharma said, giving them a slight frown as though they'd just missed a bus. "I suppose we'll have to find you another mirkirrado."

The two Calabi started walking down the street. Shocked, Milo said "Wait a minute! Didn't you see that thing? Shouldn't we report this to someone?"

"Report it? Of course not. The emergency services are already on their way. They'll take care of everything," Sensen Dharma said.

"Ah well," Dani added, "accidents happen."

Milo looked over at his father, who looked back in amazement. Then, with no other choice, they followed their Calabi hosts.

Dani and her father led them down a main street. They crossed two other streets, and as they approached a third, Milo saw another white-and-green building up ahead. "There's the other mirkirrado," Dani said. "I knew it was close."

Milo barely heard her. His eyes had been drawn to a hole in a tall building to their left. The building itself looked normal enough. On Earth he would have called it a skyscraper and guessed that it held lots of offices. The strange thing was, a huge tunnel went right through the middle of it. The tunnel was almost two stories high and perfectly round.

Looking down the tunnel, Milo could see that it passed completely through the building. On the far side, he glimpsed the next street over. Beyond that was another building with another tunnel, and so on for blocks.

Glancing to his right, Milo saw that the buildings on that side of the street had a series of tunnels, too.

"Is this some sort of mass transit system, like a railway?" he asked out loud.

Dani glanced at the small digital device on her wrist. "Oh, excuse me. Step back please." She tugged on Milo's shirt until he stepped back.

An instant later, Milo heard the same shriek, felt the same blast of hot air, and was blinded by the same bright light. He managed to keep his feet this time, but the light was too intense for him not to squint when the thing passed by. It was gone in an instant, just as before. Only this time no buildings had been destroyed. Instead the light ball had passed through the tunnels.

"Well," Dani said with a smile, "at least some things are as normal as ever. This way, please!"

—

The Calabi led them to the mirkirrado, where a courteous desk clerk checked them into a room. A bellhop then took their bags and showed them to the autolift that would carry them to their sleeping chamber.

Dani and her father walked them to the autolift, where they all shook hands again. "I have a few things to finish back at my workstation," Sensen Dharma said. "But it is still early. Perhaps we could meet after midday for a visit to the Geothermal Tap?"

"Sounds good," Hal Forecastle agreed. "Um, in the meantime, should we be watching out for any more of those, uh, light balls?"

Sensen Dharma looked at him oddly, then glanced down at the timepiece he wore on his wrist. "Not for hours to come," he replied. Then he and Dani excused themselves.

As the autolift carried the humans up to their room, Milo questioned his dad: "What were those things? What's going on here?"

"I don't think I can answer the second question," his dad confessed. "But as to the first—they were energy spheres of some kind. Pure energy. And from the looks of those tunnels we saw, they come through the city on a regular basis."

"One of those things killed a building full of people, and the Calabi didn't seem to care."

His dad shrugged. "Keep your mind on the job, Milo. We're here to help them fix their geothermal tap, and that's all."

"Well, it's going to be pretty tough to fix anything if we get wiped out by one of those energy balls," Milo grumbled. He spotted a vidscreen on the wall. Finding the remote, he turned it on. The screen lit up with scribbles that must have been the

Calabi written language. Then the scribbles faded out and were replaced by Standard, the common language of the galaxy.

> WELCOME TO OUR ILLUSTRIOUS MIRKIRRADO!
> FOR YOUR PLEASURE, THE WATER HAS BEEN WARMED TO A TEMPERATURE COMFORTABLE FOR YOUR SPECIES.
> THE WEATHER TODAY WILL BE WARM AND SUNNY. WE'RE IN FOR A PARTICULARLY BEAUTIFUL SUNSET TONIGHT, WITH LIGHT DUSTING FROM THE ASTEROID BELT ADDING A SPARKLE TO THE SKY.
> PLASMA SPHERE ALPHA IS ON NORMAL COURSE AND SCHEDULE.
> PLASMA SPHERE BETA IS OFF COURSE AND OFF TIME BY 13 SECONDS. PLEASE BE ALERT IF YOU ARE WITHIN ONE-HALF MILE OF ITS PREVIOUS PATH.
> PLASMA SPHERE GAMMA IS ON NORMAL COURSE AND SCHEDULE.
> HAVE A NICE DAY!

"Plasma sphere," Milo read. That must be what the Calabi called those violent energy balls that had wiped out a building. Were they part of some schedule? What exactly was going on here?

A short time later, Milo and his father had changed out of their flight gear and into civilian clothes. Returning to the lobby they found Sensen Dharma and Dani waiting with a hovercar nearby. They all got in and the car lifted into the sky, zipping toward the outskirts of the city. Eventually it set down near a huge geothermal plant.

But instead of going into the plant, Sensen Dharma led them to an open area beyond the plant. There stood a large domed building with several round openings—like the tunnels in the buildings they'd seen earlier that day. Milo could see huge machines inside.

Beyond the dome, Milo noticed a curious thing: a field of blackened ground that had been burned smooth, like dark glass.

"I'm afraid Dr. Forecastle and I must talk business," Sensen Dharma said. "Perhaps you young ones could go for a walk?"

"Actually," Milo's dad said, "my son might be interested in—"

"It's okay, Dad," Milo said. "You go ahead."

The two adults went into the big domed building.

"Fathers," Milo said. "My dad's always pushing me to become like him."

Dani laughed and her tail lashed out playfully. "I guess they're alike on every planet. Mine has already decided I'm going to be a diplomat."

It was Milo's turn to laugh. "What do you want to be?" he asked.

"Right now I'm trying to convince father I'd be the worst diplomat in the galaxy!" She looked at him mischievously. "I hope you didn't mind that kiss. I knew it wasn't the right thing to do, but I'm trying to show him how bad I am at diplomacy!"

They both laughed. Then Milo said, "You know, you *can* tell me something. What's that field of black glass over there? It looks like there was an explosion."

Dani nodded. "This was the site of the original geothermal plant. Then there was an accident. But it was hundreds of years ago."

"Hundreds of years ago?" Milo asked. He pointed at all the rubble lying around. "Why haven't they cleaned that up?"

Dani laughed. "The spheres still pass through here a couple of times a day. Why clean up anything when they'd just wreck it again?" She paused. "The spheres were part of the accident. You see, our scientists were trying to find a way to create unlimited energy, like a battery that never dies. They succeeded. Sort of. But something went wrong, and the three energy spheres they created broke loose of the magnetic fields that held them, and then all three exploded out of the old power plant. They've been circling the planet ever since."

Milo was stunned. "You mean, those same three energy spheres have been rolling around your planet for centuries?" He couldn't believe what he was hearing. "Why doesn't someone try to stop them?"

Dani shook her head. "You saw what one of them did to that building. *Nothing* can stop them. They burn right through the hardest metals. Lasers and explosives have no affect on them. They destroy everything that gets in their way."

Milo remembered the tunnels through the buildings. "Do they ever change course? Do people ever get hurt?"

Dani frowned. "Well, accidents do happen. A few people die every year because they forget the time or aren't paying attention to where they're standing. But what can you do? For the first hundred years the sphere paths didn't change at all.

They're really not that dangerous, you know. They only damage what they come into direct contact with. So we Calabi just plan our lives around them." She flicked her tail thoughtfully. "It's sort of in our nature. We're adaptable. The plasma spheres are here, so we adapt to them."

"What makes them change course?" Milo asked.

Dani shrugged. "Different things. Gravitational changes in the planet. A passing comet. Anything that affects gravity or magnetism." Her face brightened. "In fact, my friends and I know some nova tricks using the plasma spheres. You ever do anything really warped?"

Milo laughed. "According to my dad, all the time."

Dani twitched her tail. "If you want, I can show you in the morning."

Milo shrugged. "Sure."

Dani smiled. "Meet me in the park behind your mirkirrado tomorrow at sunrise."

———

"These people are insane!" Milo's father shouted.

They had returned to the mirkirrado for the night.

"Insane," Hal Forecastle repeated. He was pacing back and forth through the door that connected his room to Milo's. "You know, the work they want me to do here has nothing to do with the Geothermal Tap," he said.

"Yeah, you've said that several times since we got to the room," Milo pointed out.

"They want me to find a way to harness the energy of those . . . those things!" the elder Forecastle said.

Sensen Dharma had told Milo's father the same history of the plasma spheres, then added a few details. Apparently each year, nearly a thousand Calabi were killed by the spheres.

Finally, Hal Forecastle got tired of pacing and sat down on the edge of the bed. "You know, I'm not sure whether to be horrified or impressed. Milo, do you know how long intelligent beings have been searching for an energy source that would never die out? These people found it! Only they can't control it, and now people are dying."

"Are you going to help them?" Milo asked

His father heaved a sigh. "Not if I can find a way out of this project. Those plasma spheres should be destroyed, not used as any kind of energy source. They're killers."

Milo paused a moment. Then he met his father's gaze evenly. "That's against the rules, isn't it? Doesn't the Law of Preservation say you're not allowed to interefere in the lives of people outside the Trade Alliance?"

The elder Forecastle scowled. "Son, I don't need to be reminded of the rules."

Milo continued. "But I'm right, aren't I? If you choose not to help them just because you don't approve, it's like interfering. You're passing judgment on the way they live."

"I'm doing it to save lives, Milo," his father said.

Father and son stared at each other. They both knew the argument wasn't about the Calabi anymore. It was about the elder Forecastle's interference in Milo's life.

"You always have a good reason," Milo muttered.

"That's right," his father said, as always guessing what his son was really thinking. "And in your case I'm interfering because it's my job. I'm your father. The things I'm doing are for your own good." He paused. "Milo, you can make something of yourself."

"I will," Milo replied. "But it'll be what *I* want."

His father shook his head. "What do you want, son? To be a kid all your life? To play games in the streets? I want you to use your talents. That's why I keep taking you on these trips with me."

"Even though I hate to go," Milo snapped.

His father opened his mouth to reply, then took a deep breath. "You're wearing me out, Milo, and I've got a lot of work to do." He took another deep breath and said, "Looking at it like a scientist, I'd say two opposing forces are about to collide. Either one destroys the other, or they cancel each other out."

—

Milo woke early. The room next door was quiet, and Milo guessed that his father must finally be asleep. Milo had heard him up all night, tossing and turning. Sometimes he got up and paced the room. Obviously it wasn't easy for him to decide whether to break the Law of Preservation and refuse to help or to contribute to a technology that would cause more deaths.

Milo went to the window of his room and looked outside. The window looked out over an open park with wide, grassy fields. The grass on Calabi-Yau was a soft yellow, which looked nice against the purple sky. The sun was just coming up, spreading warm light over the park.

Milo could see a straight line cut through the park. At first he thought it was a road but quickly realized it was one of the plasma sphere paths. As he watched, he saw four or five figures scurrying around on the path beginning to set up a large net on sturdy poles.

That must be Dani and her friends, he thought. *But what are they doing?*

It was a short walk to the park. By the time he arrived, the Calabi had finished putting up their net. Like Dani, they were about Milo's age. As Milo approached, Dani stepped out of the crowd.

"Morning to you, Milo," she said. "Are you ready to test your courage?"

"Sure," he replied.

A young Calabi male stepped forward. Milo noticed that about a third of his tail was missing. Instead of tapering gracefully into a furred tip, it ended in a stump.

"So you're the Earther," he said. "I'm Edik."

"Milo," said Milo. "What have you got going here?"

Dani grinned. "Something very nova."

She held up a large backpack. But instead of a pouch at the back, it had six large metal rings. The rings were humming, powered by something inside the pack.

"Electromagnets," Dani said.

"What do we do with those?" he asked.

"The plasma spheres are held together by electromagnetic fields. That's like a magnetic force field that surrounds the sphere—"

"Give me a break," Milo said. "My dad's a techno-dweeb. I know all about electromagnetic fields."

"Very well," she said with a laugh. "We give these electro-magnets the same magnetic charge, which means that when the spheres come close—"

"Oh, shards," Milo whispered, figuring out what she meant. Now he knew what the net was for.

"Are you willing to try?" she asked.

"Suit me up," he replied. He yawned. "But why do you get up so early for this?"

Dani winked. "Because it's against the law. But it's also a total pulsar." *Pulsar* was standard slang for anything that was a real blast. "We call it sphere-bouncing."

A few minutes later, Milo was standing on the edge of the sphere path, wearing the magnetic backpack. The large net the Calabi had set up was about a hundred yards away. Dani and the other Calabi had also put on backpacks, and they were lined up in the middle of the path, facing the net. About 10 yards separated each person.

Dani guided Milo to the front of the line. "Stay here and duck down as low as you can."

"Why?" Milo asked.

"Because you're going last. That means everyone else is going to be flying right over your head when the sphere reaches them."

Milo wasn't sure he liked the idea of having people hurtle over his head. "Why do I have to go last? Why can't I go first and fly over other people?"

Dani smiled. "Okay. But that means when you hit the net you'll have four people coming right behind you. If you don't get out of the way quick enough, you'll get smashed. Or you'll end up as charred as the tip of Edik's tail."

Milo frowned. "Oh, this sounds like *lots* of fun."

Dani checked her timepiece. "The sphere will be through here in a few minutes. Just let the magnets do their work and you'll get the ride of your life."

Milo felt a familiar warm breeze. The plasma sphere was approaching! He crouched down and glanced behind him. About 50 yards back he saw the first of the Calabi kids stand up. It was Edik. Beyond him, Milo could see the glowing yellow ball of the energy sphere.

Edik looked over his shoulder as the ball approached. His feet pranced nervously as the ball grew closer and closer until, tall as a house, it barreled down on the group gathered at the net. It was so bright that Edik became a dark silhouette against it.

Squinting against the light, Milo tried to keep watching. He barely saw Edik brace himself, and then suddenly the Calabi launched into the air as if pulled forward by a giant string. Milo ducked and felt the Calabi pass over his head like a missile, with a cry of "Yeeeeeeeahhhhhhahhhahhha!"

Milo then heard a second Calabi shout as he, too, was launched into the air by the force of the magnets meeting the sphere. Then a third flew past. Then a fourth.

By this time the heat and noise of the sphere were intense. Milo jumped to his feet and braced himself.

Suddenly he was flying through the air. Wind whipped past his face and pulled the tears right out of his eyes. He was sure he'd left his stomach back at the sphere as he flew at hyperspeed a dozen feet off the ground. A split second of sheer terror was followed by an electric sense of excitement.

And then it was over. He slammed into the large net, which was flexible enough to give as he landed. He lay against the net for a minute, then started laughing. "Nova! Totally nova!" he yelled. "That was the best ride I've ever—"

"Move!" Dani yelled. He felt her pulling at his arm. "Get off the net! Now!"

Calabi hands dragged him off the net just in time. A moment later the sphere caught up with them, slamming through the net, which disintegrated in a flash.

Suddenly sirens wailed all around them and hovercraft appeared over the trees, multicolored lights flashing.

"Lawbringers!" Edik yelled. "Let's go hyper!"

But it was too late. They were surrounded. Six hovercraft landed in a circle around them.

The doors of one of the hovercraft opened, and out stepped Sensen Dharma and another Calabi. With dark looks on their faces they hurried toward the group of young sphere-bouncers.

The color of Dani's fur faded with worry. "Father! Father, I'm sorry, I didn't—"

"Be silent, please," Sensen Dharma said. "We'll discuss your illegal activities later. This has nothing to do with you." The Calabi turned to Milo. "We've come for you, Milo. Your father is in trouble."

———

A hovercar carrying Sensen Dharma, Milo, Dani, and the other sphere-bouncers raced through the air in the direction of the geothermal plant. Milo asked a hundred questions on the way, but all Sensen Dharma would say is there had been an accident.

A few moments later the emergency hovercar arrived at the power plant. Instead of leading them into the plant itself, Sensen Dharma led them to the field of black glass Milo had noticed the day before. The portable dome was still there, and from a distance the place looked normal. But as he approached, Milo saw a crowd of technicians gathered around one of the machines inside.

Hurrying forward, Milo saw that the machine was like a large hollow tube. It was high and wide enough to allow one of the spheres to pass through. As Sensen Dharma helped him push his way through the crowd, Milo saw his father standing inside the giant tube. His father even waved to him. The elder Forecastle looked more embarrasssed than injured.

"Hey, Dad!" Milo called out.

"He can't hear you," Sensen Dharma said. "An energy field blocks out the sound."

"What's going on?" he asked the Calabi scientist.

Sensen Dharma looked grave. "This tube is called a dynamo. We were building it to capture the energy of the spheres. Theoretically, when dynamo tubes are positioned correctly, the spheres pass right through them and the tubes draw off some of their energy. Your father came in early to work on this one. Not realizing it's still in the testing phase, he went inside. Now he's trapped."

Milo said, "Why don't you just shut the thing off?"

"Unfortunately, the device has malfunctioned," Sensen

Dharma explained. "We cannot shut it off. And we cannot move the dynamo while it's activated without . . ." he paused. "Without killing your father."

Milo's stomach churned. He had a feeling he hadn't heard the worst. "Well then, we just leave him here until we figure out a way to get him out, right?"

"I'm afraid it's more complicated than that. The plasma spheres are scheduled to arrive soon. The first one will be here in 17 minutes, the second in 18, and the third in 20. And the dynamos are all positioned in their path."

Milo felt the hairs on the back of his neck rise. His father was trapped right in the path of those spheres. He remembered the demolished mirkirrado and the burning net, and the feeling of the powerful energy globe bearing down on him.

"We've got to do something," he said. "We've got to destroy those spheres."

Sensen Dharma bowed his head. "We cannot destroy the spheres."

Milo shook his head in disbelief. "There must be some way—"

"No," Sensen Dharma said. "Young man, forgive me, but even if there were a way to destroy them, we could not. We *would* not."

"What!" Milo exclaimed.

"The plasma spheres represent enormous energy for our planet, energy we need to survive as a species. We need that energy to power our machines, our hovercraft, even the appliances in our homes. Each life is precious, but one life against the fate of an entire planet—"

"You people are crazy!" Milo yelled, echoing his father. "My dad is trapped in there and he's going to be killed, and all you can talk about is energy sources. You've been living with those spheres for so long you don't even see how terrible they are. They kill people! You're sacrificing thousands of lives every year so you can drive your hovercars!"

Sensen Dharma stiffened. "Do you know your Earth's history? Is what we do so different from your own past? For hundreds of years, human beings used fossil fuels—I believe you referred to them as 'oil'—to power your cars and your factories. Those fossil fuels polluted the skies and raised the temperature on your planet. Then you switched to nuclear power. Your nuclear power plants created radioactive waste that killed many people and caused diseases in others."

"Well, that was—"

Sensen Dharma continued. "What would you say, young man, if I offered your people a means of transportation that allowed them to travel great distances. However, this device would kill 20,000 people every year."

"I'd say forget it," Milo snapped.

"And yet for hundreds of years you humans drove automobiles, and thousands died in automobile crashes every year—"

"Okay, okay!" Milo interrupted. "I get your point. Humans have done stupid things. But our stupid things don't make your stupid things all right!"

Milo looked at his father. Although no one had been able to communicate with him there inside the dynamo tube, Hal

Forecastle had seen the concerned looks on everyone's face and he knew something was terribly wrong.

Milo felt guilt tear at his heart. His father had gotten up early to come work on the energy project. Had he decided to help the Calabi because of what Milo had said? Was he, Milo, responsible for this?

"I'm going to save him!" Milo shouted. "There's got to be a way to save him!"

Sensen Dharma said, "Milo, even if we wanted to destroy the spheres, there is simply no way. All three spheres are headed in this direction. At this site, they pass within about 10 or 15 yards of one another. According to our satellite tracking, one will pass harmlessly to the side. But the other two will both pass close enough to destroy the dynamo. We're working hard to find a way to get your father out, but—"

The Calabi went on, but Milo wasn't listening. His mind had drifted back to his conversation with his father. Something in the conversation nagged at him. Something that seemed important. Something his father had said . . .

Suddenly he said softly, "Two opposing forces that collide. Either one destroys the other, or they cancel each other out."

"Excuse me?" Sensen Dharma said.

"Nothing," Milo said. But to himself, he added, *I just figured out how to stop the spheres.*

—

While Sensen Dharma and the other Calabi technicians continued looking for a way to shut down the dynamo tube, Milo found his way back to where the emergency vehicles were parked. Piled in front of him were the electromagnetic back-packs. He'd managed to convince the sphere-bouncers to give them all to him. Picking up one, he opened the pack and started working on the wiring inside.

Dani watched him and looked impressed. "I didn't realize you knew so much about science."

"Yeah, my dad wants me to become an energineer," Milo said as he worked. "There." He held up the pack.

"What did you do?" she asked.

"I reversed the magnetic fields," he explained.

Dani raised an eyebrow. "But that means we can't use it to sphere-bounce anymore. Instead of bouncing us away from the sphere it would—"

"Pull the sphere toward you," he said.

Edik stepped up to him and pointed to his timepiece. "The spheres are coming."

Quickly, Milo reversed the magnetic fields in the other four backpacks as well. Then he strapped all five to his body.

Milo looked up. From three different directions, the huge energy globes appeared, rolling straight toward the dome.

"Are you sure you know what you're doing, Milo?" Dani asked.

"No," he said. He managed a smile. "But it's going to be nova."

Without another word, he trotted out onto the field of blackened glass. At the center of the field, he studied the approaching plasma spheres.

They were close.

When they were about 200 yards away, Milo could already

tell which one would pass by harmlessly. He ignored that one and looked at the other two. One was approaching from his left, the other from his right, and the power dome lay right where they would pass close to each other.

Somehow Milo had to draw one of the spheres off its path and get it to strike the other.

Milo chose the closest one, the one on his left. All he had to do was stand on the side of the path. As the sphere passed by, the magnets would draw it off its old course and put it on a new one—one that would lead it toward the other energy globe. Maybe nothing on the planet could destroy a plasma sphere, but what happened when one sphere met another?

Milo planted himself near the path of the sphere and waited.

A moment later he realized the flaw in his plan.

Still wearing the magnets, he felt a tug at the backpack straps. The plasma sphere had reached the outer edge of the magnets' reach. Within seconds the tug became a strong pull. Milo had to brace his feet.

He realized he was going to die.

Yes, his plan worked perfectly: The magnets attracted the plasma sphere. The problem was, Milo was attached to the magnets.

"Oh, shards!" he said as the pull of the magnet increased. As hard as he fought, he couldn't help but take another step toward the sphere.

The sphere probably outweighed him by several tons. He wasn't drawing the sphere. The sphere was drawing him!

Simple science, he heard his dad's voice say.

As the sphere drew closer, Milo felt a giant hand haul him forward. He fell onto his back and felt himself dragged along the ground. "Help!" he called out, but there was no one to help.

His fingers clawed at the ground for something to hold onto. But the explosion hundreds of years ago had so smoothed the ground that he slid along it like a wheel on a greased track.

The roar and heat of the sphere increased.

He was going to die.

Suddenly a shadow fell over him. Milo looked up. One of the lawbringer hovercars appeared overhead, following him as he slid along the ground. Suddenly he saw Edik poke his head out of one side of the vehicle. Dani leaned out the other side. "Hold on, Milo!" she called.

"I'm trying!" he yelled back. He was picking up speed, sliding ever faster toward the approaching sphere. His skin was starting to burn from the friction.

Over the roaring of the sphere and the sputtering of the hovercar engines, Milo heard Dani yell to Edik, "Can you get this thing lower?"

"No problem!" the other Calabi said with a grin.

The hovercraft dropped so suddenly that Milo thought it would crush him. Instead it dropped to within a foot and a half of the ground, cruising right past him. Then it suddenly stopped. The hovercraft door popped open and Dani leaned out. "Grab me!" she yelled.

As he slid past, Milo grabbed Dani's outstretched hands. He felt her fingers wrap around his wrists. He stopped sliding. But the pull of the sphere was so strong, he was lifted off his feet.

His hand started to slip from Dani's grasp. Edik leaned over next to Dani and he, too, grabbed hold of Milo.

"We have to pull that thing off course!" Milo shouted. He gritted his teeth. He was sure his arms would be pulled right out from their sockets.

"It's too strong!" Dani yelled.

Desperately, Milo shook one hand loose from Dani's grip and grabbed the hovercar's crash net. Like the straps in the *Never Better,* this crash net was designed to be unbreakable. He wound his free arm around it and said, "Okay, let go now!"

Dani and Edik released him and scrambled out of the hovercar. Milo was still being pulled off his feet. The backpacks were dug into his skin, the magnets inside them irresistibly drawn to the massive sphere.

"Yahhhhhhhhrrr!" he yelled in pain. But he wouldn't let go. His father's life depended on it.

"It's working!" Dani yelled. "The sphere shifted off course."

Then the hovercraft slid. The sphere's magnetic power was drawing the magnets, which drew along Milo, who held onto the hovercar! Milo knew he couldn't hold on much longer. His hands were losing their strength. His arms felt like rubber. He had to let go.

At that moment, Dani appeared at his side. Her hands reached for the backpack straps. One by one she snapped them open, and one by one the backpacks flew through the air and were sucked into the plasma sphere. They vanished with tiny flamebursts.

Once the last backpack was released, Milo fell to the ground, exhausted. "I . . . I couldn't do it . . ." he muttered.

"Milo, you did do it!" Dani said. "Look!"

He sat up. The plasma sphere had rolled past them, unstoppable as ever. But Milo could see that it had changed course. The magnets had pulled it off track!

He watched the sphere roll steadily toward the dome, where now even Sensen Dharma had departed. But instead of heading into the building, the plasma sphere passed alongside it, singeing the outer wall but leaving everything inside, including Dr. Forecastle, unharmed.

As the sphere passed, Milo could see the second globe bearing down on it.

"Collision course!" Milo cheered.

The two spheres hurtled toward each another.

Forty yards from the dome, the two spheres struck. The force of the collision released a huge blast of energy. Heat and light shot out in every direction, and human and Calabi alike dropped to the ground, covering their ears.

The explosion was over in a heartbeat. Looking up, Milo saw no smoke, no clouds of dust, no falling debris. Pure energy, the spheres had spent all their power on each other.

—

It took a full day to release Dr. Forecastle from the dynamo tube. He emerged hungry, thirsty, and totally unaware of what had happened outside the dome. But when he heard what Milo had done, he threw his arms around the younger Forecastle.

"I told you you'd make a great energineer!" he laughed.

Milo laughed. "I told you I'd make a great daredevil video star!" His smile faded as he glanced at the Calabi around them. "I think they're upset I destroyed their spheres."

Sensen Dharma, who stood nearby, frowned. "We are . . . disappointed. But I suspect, Milo, that you saved us from committing a terrible crime. It is horrible to lose a life. In fact, we will now try to find a way to destroy the third sphere." Sensen Dharma looked at Dr. Forecastle. "I hope you will forgive us."

Dr. Forecastle shrugged. He was too happy to be alive to care. "As long as it turned out all right." He laughed weakly. "But I think you'll have to hire a new energineer. I've spent enough time with those dynamo tubes!"

"Speaking of which," Milo said, "how'd you get stuck in their in the first place, Dad?"

His father shrugged. "Accidents happen."

Y3K

ew Year's Eve? What's that?" Jemima McDonald asked the teacher.

The teacher smiled back at the class. "I'll bet Katie Single can tell us. Katie, will you tell the class, please?"

Katie rolled her eyes. She *always* got picked to answer questions like that. It wasn't fair.

Well, there was no getting around it. She was the only student who knew the answer. "New Year's Eve was a holiday celebrated hundreds of years ago, as far back as the 20th century. People used to get together and throw big parties where they wore costumes with pointy hats." While she spoke, the teacher pressed a button on her desk panel. The computer in front of each child bleeped, and an image of people wearing party hats appeared on the screens.

Ralph Gap asked, "What's that in their hands? A weapon?"

"Yeah, it looks like a T-37 laser pistol," said another boy.

"No," Katie said. "Those aren't weapons. They're noise-makers. I think they were used to scare away evil spirits."

"Did people still believe in evil spirits in the 20th century, Miss Starbucks?" Jemima McDonald asked.

The teacher thought a moment. "It was a very primitive time," she said. "After all, they didn't have anti-grav sleds yet. They drove around on vehicles with wheels."

An image of an SUV showed on each student's computer screen. "And to fuel those vehicles they used oil made from extinct dinosaurs—that was before we revived the dinosaurs, of course," Miss Starbucks continued. "And people hadn't even flown to Mars, let alone another galaxy . . ."

Katie reached down and pressed the "mute" button on her computer terminal. Instantly her teacher's lecture was cut off.

Katie Single wasn't actually *in* the classroom. That's because there was no classroom. Her entire seventh grade class met over computers all linked to Miss Starbucks's computer. Some of her classmates Katie hadn't even met in person. At least one of them lived in India but telecommuted to Katie's class in the Americas.

"Command interrupt," chirped her computer. "Katie, are you with us?" asked Miss Starbucks on the computer screen. Katie straightened. Although she could mute the class, during school hours her teacher had ultimate control over the command program.

"Yes, sorry," Katie lied. "I hit the 'mute' by mistake."

"All right," the teacher said. "I was just telling the class that, by old Earth standards, this is a very special New Year's

Eve. It's the end of the millennium. The third millennium, to be exact."

Ralph Gap jumped in. " 'Millennium' means 'one thousand,' so I suppose the reference is to a thousand years. But what's so special about that?"

"Katie?" the teacher asked.

Katie stifled a groan. She knew the teacher was only trying to encourage her. Katie was usually quiet and soft-spoken in class. But she was also an expert on ancient Earth traditions, and this was Miss Starbucks's way of bringing her out of her shell.

"Way back then, people thought every thousand years was significant. At the end of the second millennium, they all thought the power would go out."

"Power go out?" Ralph said. "What's that mean?"

"Well," Miss Starbucks explained, "that means everything stops working."

Jemima laughed. "That's impossible."

Katie added, "Some people thought the world would end."

"The world end!" repeated Jemima McDonald. "Maybe we should all take a hypership to my mom's cabin on Jupiter."

"It's not really going to end," said Katie. "That's just an old superstition."

"Yes, Katie's right," said the teacher. "But for homework, I want you all to write an essay on ancient Earth. I expect your essays to be uploaded to me by tomorrow morning. Have a nice day!"

An electronic school bell clanged out of the speaker on Katie's computer, signaling the end of class. Her screen went black, but then a small image box popped up in the corner, showing Jemima's face.

"Hey, Katie, can you help me with my paper?"

Before she could reply, Ralph Gap's face popped up in another little window. "Hey, Katie, can you help me with my paper?"

"Sure," she groaned. "Meet me outside, on the commons."

Katie got up from her desk and stretched. Then she maneuvered her way through the mess in her bedroom, kicking old clothes to the side and wading through a pile of empty food-wrap strips. Her father forbid her to eat food-wrap meals, but he also respected her privacy. So she secretly bought them and hid them under her bed. Food-wrap meals weren't as good as the home-cooked meals her father prepared, but if she didn't eat them like her friends did, she would have felt like even more of an oddball.

As Katie left her room, her shoulders tensed up. Her bedroom looked like the room of any normal human being living at the end of the 30th century. But walking out her door was like walking through a time machine into the past. The floors in the hallway were made of wood—real wood! And the walls were covered with pictures taken on a kind of paper called film.

She walked through the musty living room full of antiques and into her father's workshop. The heart of the time warp.

The workshop was filled with a soft *sh-sh-sh* sound, and the air was alive with flying dust. Her father was bent over a large metal device that held a long piece of wood. As he pumped a pedal on the floor, the device made the piece of wood turn around and around. As the wood turned, her father shaved it with a sharp blade. From years of experience, she could tell he was making a piece of furniture. Probably a chair.

Her father was absolutely the only person in the world who earned a living this way. He made things by hand. The fact that he *made* anything at all was unusual in his day, when everyone's wants were met by machines. He was an absolute oddball.

Seeing Katie, her father stood up straight. "Quick," he said. "How do you make bread?"

Answering automatically, Katie said, "Plant a grain like wheat or rye. Sow in the spring, harvest in the fall. Crush the grain into a fine powder called flour. Mix with water and yeast, and bake it in an oven."

"And how do you make an oven?" her father asked.

She sighed. What a day this was becoming. "Mix clay into a large hollow mound. Build a fire inside and bake the clay until hard. Then, over the fire, place a screen or something else. Lay the bread on this and light the fire. Cook until the outside is brown."

Her father nodded. "You know your stuff."

"Yeah, I didn't have much choice," she muttered under her breath. Louder she said, "I'm going outside to meet Jemima and Ralph."

"Outside, good!" her father intoned. "Always good to go outside. I'm surprised you're dragging those lazy slugs out of their shells. Now, out with you!" he joked.

Surprised that she'd gotten away so easily, she bolted for the door. But just as she reached it she heard his voice behind her: "How do you find which way is north?"

Without turning around, she called out, "Moss grows on the north side of trees. The North Star is the brightest in the sky. Put a bit of magnetized metal on a piece of wood, float this on water, and the metal will spin toward the north!"

Then she slipped out.

All the time, she thought as she left the house and walked onto the green lawn of their yard. *All the time he asks me about that old-fashioned stuff. I'm getting tired of it!*

Their green lawn blended seamlessly into the green lawns of other houses to form a wide, grassy park the locals called the commons. Such spaces were typical these days. Centuries ago, she knew, the spaces between houses were paved over to make roads for automobiles, but ever since the invention of the anti-grav sled in the 25th century, roads had become obsolete.

Jemima McDonald and Ralph Gap appeared out of their houses too. They blinked in the sunlight. Preferring to spend time indoors, in front of computers and entertainment screens, they didn't get out much.

They waved and walked over to where Katie stood. Both kids carried DAs with them—that is, digital assistants, or small devices that kept track of everything for them.

"Thanks for helping us," Ralph said. "You know everything about that useless old stuff."

"Tell me about it," Katie said. "And my dad wants me to learn more. Last week we went fishing."

"Fishing?" Jemima said. "What's that?"

Katie explained that it involved tying a piece of string to a sharp hook and dropping the hook into the water, then waiting for a fish to bite. When a fish got hooked, you hauled it up and skinned it.

"You're lying," Jemima said, aghast.

"Nope," Katie said. "I actually had to do it."

"Oh, you poor dear," the other girl said.

Ralph said, "Let's get started."

"Yeah," Jemima replied. "You can tell us more while we walk to a food-wrappery. I'm starved."

Ralph poked a command into his DA. "I know a good one. It's this way. Down by the Dinosaur Menagerie."

South, Katie thought automatically as they walked along the green lawns.

"So, Katie," Jemima asked, "why does your dad make you learn all that stuff?"

"I dunno," she replied. "Waste of time if you ask me. But he's into all that old-fashioned junk. He says I ought to learn everything the people in ancient times learned."

As they walked, Katie answered their questions about ancient Earth—thousands of years ago when human beings sailed *on* the water instead of *over* it. When people thought space flight was impossible instead of flying to distant galaxies just to have lunch.

"No offense, Katie, but who needs to know all that?" Jemima asked. "Everything I need to know is right here." She tapped her DA.

They passed a set of wide gates. In the distance, they could hear roars and grunts and squeals. The Dinosaur Menagerie. But the gates were closed.

"Oh, g'dang!" Ralph said. "I wanted to stop in and see the dinosaurs. I was going to write about them."

Jemima shuddered. "No way you're getting me in there. It's just as easy to check them out over the computer."

Ralph consulted his DA. "Yeah, the Dinosaur Menagerie closes at midnight." He looked up at the bright sun. "The sun's still up. I didn't know it was that late."

Jemima laughed. "What a deadhead! You should check your DA more often. It said on the weather report they were keeping the sun on until midnight tonight."

That was another thing, Katie thought. In the old days, before human beings had mastered gravity, they lived at the whim of nature. They had to survive cold winters and hot summers, flooding and drought. But hundreds of years ago they learned to control the weather, and gravity engines moved the planet however human beings chose. Which meant they could make the sun shine for 24 hours whenever they wanted.

Ralph was still frowning. On the other side of the gate, some enormous monster howled hungrily. "There's no danger, of course," he said. "All the dinosaurs are kept behind energy screens. They can't get free."

As they spoke, the sun finally began to fade. The planet's programmers were turning off the daylight. It was twilight now. Automatic lights popped on all over the city.

Jemima looked at Katie. "What are you going to write about?"

"How useless it is to know this stuff," Katie responded without hesitation. "We're living in the 31st century. Who needs to know how to bake bread? Or which way is north?"

Just then, an atomic clock in a building miles away clicked over a notch.

Every timekeeper on the planet was tied into that one atomic clock. So at that same moment, billions of clocks all over the world clicked over as well. It was precisely 12:00:00 A.M., January 1, 3000, everywhere in the world.

And at 12:00:01 A.M., every single clock in the world shut down.

So did every anti-grav sled and every computer.

And so did everything else, from the mighty gravity engines that controlled the planet to the tiny DAs in the palms of their hands.

The world went dark.

Jemima screamed. Ralph Gap shrieked. In the dark around them, other voices cried out in alarm. A whole city that had never known anything but comfort and convenience found itself paralyzed.

Answering those screams came growls and snarls from beyond the gates. Inside the Dinosaur Menagerie, creatures belonging to the past roared as if sensing they might have a future.

"What's happened?" Ralph shouted. "Where'd the lights go?"

Jemima was punching commands into her DA. "It's not answering me," she wailed.

"It's not working," Katie said. Panic threatened to over-whelm her, but she tried to stay calm. She heard another, louder howl from behind the dinosaur gates. "We should get away from this place. We should go home."

"Great!" Ralph said. Without thinking, he punched codes into his DA and got no response. "But how do we get home? I don't know the way without my DA!"

Jemima started to cry. Something huge leaned against the dinosaur gate, testing its strength.

Katie looked around, her terror growing. Then she looked up. And gasped.

Above her, thousands of lights had suddenly become visible. It was the light of stars. Of course she'd seen stars before, many times. She'd even visited a few on field trips. But to see them suddenly light up, free of the mask of city lights and satellites, she was awestruck at how incredibly bright they shone, just as she'd read about in ancient books.

And one of them shone brighter than the others, so much brighter that at first Katie thought it was a starship. But it wasn't. It twinkled at her. And she knew which one it was.

In the dark she grabbed the hands of her two friends. "Come on," she said. "This way."

Flight

"You know," Uncle Horis said to Wilber, "they banished your father for acting like this."

Wilber sat huddled over his desk. He raised his hands up over his head to shut out his uncle's voice. The wide leather flaps that hung from his forearms to his hips covered him like a blanket.

"Well, maybe if I'm lucky I'll get banished too," Wilber said spitefully. "It can't be any worse than living here."

Uncle Horis's face went pale. He hurried forward, waving his hands as if to slap the words right out of the air. "Don't say that, Wilber, don't ever say that! The southern continent is a horrible place to live. There isn't a day I don't wish your father back home."

Wilber's uncle sighed. "You know, Wilber, your father had a chance to go into the bezza oil business with me. I make good money. Your father could have been a huge success. He was smart."

He was *too* smart, Wilber thought. But he didn't say anything. There was no use arguing with his uncle. Horis meant well.

"And you, too, Wilber," his uncle continued. "You've got brains on top of that beak. You could join me in the business someday. All you have to do is come by the factory and learn."

"Thanks, Uncle Horis. I'll think about it."

"In the meantime," the older Hodar said, "please, Wilber, promise me you won't show that to anyone else."

Wilber was saved from answering by the jingle of a bell rising up from the bottom floor of the house. Someone was at the door. Uncle Horis turned away, leaving Wilber to stare at the small, intricate object on his desk.

The object was about the size of Wilber's hand. Three sets of slats ran perpendicular through the middle of its long, narrow body. The whole device rested on two sets of tiny wheels that turned when Wilber pushed it. Most impressively, if he tugged at a superthin string running along the model's bottom, the three sets of slats rose up and down. They moved like wings, which was exactly what they were. The device was . . .

". . . a flying machine," Wilber breathed. He said the words with a sense of awe. It seemed impossible. But his father had been so sure flight was possible. And Wilber knew how smart his father was. He just had to be right.

Unfortunately for Wilber's father, their people, the Hodarii, were convinced otherwise. The Hodarii had tried to fly for centuries, but every experiment ended in failure. Hundreds of lives had been lost until the Hodarii central council, the Aerie, forbid any further experiments. From then on, the subject of air flight was taboo. Any Hodar convicted of conducting experiments in air flight was banished to the southern continent. There a colony of settlers and convicts scratched out a meager living growing fruit in the poor soil.

Wilber raised his arms and flapped his wings uselessly. "But it's ridiculous," he muttered. "Why would we have been born with wings if we weren't meant to fly?"

"I dunno," came a voice from the doorway. "Why does my dad keep telling me the same old stories over and over again?"

Wilber turned to see his best friend, Orville. Orville strolled into the room and dropped a package on Wilber's worktable, then flopped down on Wilber's bed, his long beak pointed toward the ceiling. Wilber's dad had theorized that the Hodars' birdlike beaks, like their wings, were proof that flying was their birthright. Of that, Wilber wasn't so sure. Their beaks looked more like the long mouths of alligators.

"What does this have to do with your dad?" Wilber asked.

"Nothing," Orville laughed. "It's just that he keeps telling me lame old stories. Why? I dunno. Just like you don't know the answer to your question."

Wilber frowned. "You're saying that my dad's also been telling me lame old stories?"

Orville sat up and shrugged. "I don't mean to slam your dad. It's just that . . . well, didn't he also tell you that someday we'd be able to fly into outer space? That we'd visit alien cultures and stuff?"

"Yeah," Wilber admitted.

"Yeah, well, that's just as crazy as thinking Hodarii can fly."

Seeing Wilber start to sulk, Orville tried to lighten things up. "Speaking of aliens," he said, half jokingly, "you hear about the meteor last night?"

"No," Wilber said. "I was too busy working on my model flying machine."

"It was amazing," his friend said. "Bright as all three moons put together, it zipped down over the forest just on the other side of the cliffs. And landed with a huge boom. I'm surprised you didn't hear it."

Wilber did hear something the night before, but since few exciting things ever happened among the Hodarii, he'd figured it wasn't worth investigating.

"You're just like everyone else," Wilber said defensively. "If aliens landed right in the middle of the town square, you'd probably throw rocks at them."

Orville frowned, and Wilber instantly regretted his harsh words. "Look," Orville said. "I'm still your friend, aren't I? I'm just saying that even if you love your dad, you've got to look at both sides . . ."

Wilber interrupted him. "What's this?" he asked, pointing to the package his friend had dropped.

"The mail came right when I got here," Orville said. "Looks like it's from your dad."

Wilber tore open the package. He wasn't expecting to find anything exciting inside. The authorities censored all mail from the southern continent. But Wilber didn't care. Just getting a package from his father was a treat. It made him feel the connection between father and son, despite the thousands of miles separating them.

Inside, Wilber found a handwritten note and a small pile of bachii fruit. The note said simply: *Dear Wilber, just a few sweets to keep your spirits soaring. Love, Dad.* But those few words were enough to fill the young Hodar with joy.

Wilber picked up one of the yellowish, fuzzy-skinned bachii fruit and tossed it to his friend. Orville caught and scowled. "Bachii fruit? No thanks. I'd rather bite a shoe."

Wilber laughed. "Suit yourself." Bachii fruit weren't all that tasty—but they were from his dad. He bit into one and felt the juice trickle down his beak. Eating the fruit was like absorbing bits of his father's life. Somewhere across the ocean, his father the genius was scraping a paltry life out of the soil. These fruits were the result. He would have eaten them even if they'd tasted 10 times as bad.

Seeing how much his friend relished the bachii, Orville groaned. "All right, all right," he said. He bit into the fruit. "Oh, drek!" he muttered. "It's worse than I thought. This tastes like paper!"

Orville pulled the fruit out of his mouth. To his surprise, he found that he'd bitten into more than just bachii fruit. "Hey, it *is* paper."

"What?" Wilber asked.

Orville held up a half-chewed scrap. Wilber snatched it and the rest of the fruit from his friend's hand. Looking at the fruit closely, he saw that a tiny hole had been drilled near the stem. The paper had been tightly rolled and slipped inside.

Unrolling it quickly, Wilber felt his heart pound. It was a note from his father. An uncensored note.

Dear Wilber,

I hope this letter finds you well. Life here is harsh, but I'm getting by. I'm healthy in body, so don't worry about me. The worst part is being forbidden to try my experiments. That's why I'm risking sending this note.

I realized something important, son. All this time, I was wrong . . .

"Wilber, what are you doing?"

The young Hodar's heart leaped into his throat. His uncle was standing over him, glowering. He snatched the note from Wilber's hand. "An illegal note!" The older Hodar wouldn't even look at it. "Blasphemy!"

"It's mine!" Wilber demanded.

"It's against the law!" his uncle retorted. He ripped the note in half, then ripped it into illegible shreds.

"No!" Wilber gasped.

Instantly, Uncle Horis's voice softed. "Wilber, I . . . I'm sorry. I didn't mean to be so harsh. But . . . but you could be banished too . . ."

"I wish I were!" Rushing past his uncle, the young Hodar raced out of the room.

—

Wilber didn't stop running until he reached his favorite thinking spot. It was about a half mile out of his Hodar village, up a winding trail to the top cliffs. The village was built about halfway up the gentle slope of a mountain. The mountain's far side was sheer as a wall, dropping off steeply down to the floor of a forest valley. The view from the cliffs was spectacular. As a young Hodar, Wilber had come here many times with his father.

"You feel that breeze, Wilber?" his father would say. *"Someday we'll ride that wind. Someday we'll fly."*

But that wasn't true. His father had given up. Wilber hadn't been able to read the rest of the note, but what else could his father have meant? *All this time, I was wrong . . .*

Wilber heard footsteps behind him. He knew who it was. Only Orville would know to look for him here. Without saying a word, his friend sat down, carrying a small sack. "I brought the rest of the bachii fruit. In case you wanted any."

Wilber scowled. Right now, they'd probably just taste sour in his mouth. "Maybe later."

Orville wrinkled his forehead, searching for something encouraging to say. At the same time his eyes scanned the forest. Something bright glinted, reflecting the sunlight. "What's that?" he exclaimed.

———

The path down the cliffs was steep and narrow. Over the years the ever cautious Hodarii had built handrails and steps into the path. But even with those aides it was slow going.

An hour later, the two Hodarii reached the bottom and walked into the woods. Only dappled sunlight reached through the ceiling of branches and leaves.

"Are you sure it was this way?" Wilber asked.

"How should I know?" Orville grunted, pushing a branch out of his way. "I can barely see two feet ahead of me."

Wilber pushed ahead. "We must be headed in the right direction, but that gleam didn't seem so far away."

The young Hodar climbed over a fallen log. As his foot reached for the ground, he felt it slip. Suddenly he was sliding headlong down a steep slope. "Watch it!" he called out. But it was too late. Orville tumbled down after him.

The ride was rough but short. The two friends came to an abrupt stop at the bottom of a wide, shallow crater. Above them the tree branches had been cleared away in a wide circle, as if a hole had been punched through the forest canopy.

But that wasn't what interested Wilber.

What caught his attention was the thing that had stopped his slide.

Wilber had come to rest on top of a perfectly round metal ball. An *enormous* perfectly round metal ball. The size of a Hodar house, it shone in the sun like silver.

"This is the weirdest meteor I've ever seen," Orville said.

"Like you've seen a lot of meteors," Wilber snorted.

"Well, I know they aren't supposed to look like this," the other Hodar snapped.

True, Wilber thought. The orb was half buried in the ground. Walking around the upper half, he and Orville looked for some marking on the surface.

There was nothing. Not a mark, not a scratch, not a seam. Nothing. It was as flawless as a giant marble.

"I wonder what it is," Orville said.

"I don't know," Wilber said. "But we should probably go back and tell the village elders."

"Okay," Orville agreed, "but I've got to rest a minute." He sat down at the edge of the orb and fanned himself with one leathery wing. With the other he lifted up the sack he'd been carrying all this time and asked, "You mind if I have one of these bachii fruit? *That's* how hungry I am right now."

"Sure, go ahead."

Orville pulled out a fruit and bit into it. Instantly a scowl crossed his face. "I can't believe it! This one tastes just like paper too . . ." His voice trailed off as he pulled yet another piece of paper out of his mouth.

Faster than a thought, Wilber snatched it from his grasp and unrolled it. It was another letter from his father, and it began just like the last one.

Dear Wilber,

I hope this letter finds you well. Life here is harsh, but I'm getting by. I'm healthy in body, so don't worry about me. The worst part is being forbidden to try my experiments. That's why I'm risking sending this note.

I realized something important, son. All this time, I was wrong about my research. Because we Hodar, like birds, have wings we can flap, I assumed that was the way we should fly.

But I was wrong. I realize that now. Our flight must be different. Unlike birds, we can't generate enough power to lift ourselves by flapping.

Remember the cliffs? Remember when I said we'd use that breeze someday? I think of that, every time I think of you (which is often), and that's when I realized my error. It's a waste of time to make a flapping machine. We need to make a gliding machine. But I can't do it here. There are watchful eyes and no materials. But I know how. You can do it, son. There is a piece of paper rolled in with this one. It will guide you.

All my love,

Dad

P.S.: I'm sealing this same note inside each piece of bachii fruit in case one of them is discovered.

P.P.S.: Don't get caught!

Wilber felt his heart soar higher than any flying machine could take him. His father hadn't given up! Not only that, but he'd discovered the way to succeed!

The young Hodar unrolled the other piece of paper. On it, accompanied by tiny letters, was a drawing. The drawing showed a triangle made of sheets and held together by poles. He couldn't imagine how it would work. But if his father believed it would, well, then it must.

"This is wonderful," he said aloud. "Orville, this is wonderful. Look at this."

Wilber looked up at his friend, only to realize that Orville hadn't been paying any attention to him. "Look at this, Orville," he repeated.

"Uh, no," his friend replied. "I think you should look at this."

He pointed. Wilber followed his pointing finger and gasped.

There, standing only a few feet away from them, was an alien.

—

It stood on two legs, and two arms hung from its shoulders, just like a Hodar, but the similarities stopped there. The creature was a little taller than the Hodarii, and its head was grotesque. Instead of an angular head with a long beak, the creature's head was round and its face flat. In the middle of the face was only a small bump with two small holes at the bottom. Its eyes were shaped like almonds, and little strips of fur grew over the tops. More fur grew on top of its head.

Between the fur strips above its eyes and the fur on its head, the creature's forehead appeared wounded. Liquid seemed to have spilled out of a deep cut. Wilber would have called it blood except that the liquid was red, whereas Hodar blood was yellow.

The creature took a step toward them and raised its hands. Wilber gasped. The creature had no wing flaps. There was nothing growing between its hands and body.

Freak! Wilber wanted to yell. But he choked the word down. He knew that was just how other Hodarii would react. Other Hodarii, that is, except his father.

The creature spoke, and Wilber saw two rows of small white teeth. The words themselves were gibberish, a series of grunts and hoots.

Both Hodarii sat still, frightened and unsure what to do. The creature again gestured and made sounds. Obviously, it was trying to communicate. Slowly, Wilber stood up. "Are you . . . is this orb yours?" he asked, pointing at the machine.

The creature jabbered again and pointed at itself, then at the orb, nodding. It held out a hand, said something, and waited.

Wilber didn't know what it wanted. The creature spoke again, gestured, and waited.

"What does it want?" he asked.

Orville stood up. "Is that something in its hand?"

Wilber had been so busy staring at the creature's bizarre face, he hadn't looked at its hand. It was indeed holding a small metal tube. The creature gestured again, pointed at its mouth, then at Wilber's mouth, then at the device.

"I think," he guessed, "it wants us to talk."

"Okay, what do we say?" Orville wondered.

"I don't know," Wilber said. "Maybe it's some kind of recording device. But how long are we supposed to talk?"

"That's enough."

The two Hodarii jumped back, flapping their arm-wings in fright. The voice had come out of the little device.

The creature jabbered again, and as it did the mechanical voice again came out of the little machine. "Sorry to scare you. It takes a moment for the universal translator to interpret speech patterns. But I think it's working now."

Wilber sputtered, "You mean . . . you mean you can understand us?"

He was surprised, and impressed, when the device instantly turned his speech into the grunts and hoots of the alien creature.

The creature nodded and showed its teeth, which seemed to be a sign of pleasure. "Yes, through the translator. And you can understand me."

Wilber was amazed. "Who . . . who are you?"

The creature showed its teeth again. "I'm an explorer," the machine squawked. The creature looked at it in frustration, then jabbered again. The mechanical voice said, "I am from— I am from far, far away."

"What are you called?" Orville asked.

"I am a human," the creature said.

"We are Hodarii," Wilber said. "This orb belongs to you?"

"Yes, it does. I didn't mean to bring it here. In fact, I need to leave as soon as possible."

"So what's stopping you?" Orville asked. He was clearly more frightened than Wilber.

The human walked past them and patted the orb. "I need to fix this first. But I can't repair it with the equipment I have here. I need coolant."

"What's that?" Wilber asked.

The human pointed at the orb. "When I power this up, it gets very warm. I need a liquid to run through special tubes in the shell to keep it cool."

"There's a river not too far from here," Wilber said. He was getting used to the three-way conversation: speaking, letting the machine translate, and then hearing the human's reply through the same device.

"No, water is not good," the creature said. "I need something that absorbs heat better, without boiling. Something thick, like an oil."

Wilber flapped his wings in excitement. "An oil? My uncle manufactures bezza oil. It comes from a plant. It's very thick. My people use it to lubricate our farm machines."

The human nodded excitedly. "Can we get some?"

Wilber pointed to himself and Orville. "Yes . . . well, *we* can get some. I don't think it's a good idea for you to come. My people wouldn't . . . they wouldn't react very well."

The human tilted its head to one side, signaling curiosity. "Really? You two seem to react well. I thought perhaps your species was open to the idea of—" the machine squawked again, and the creature tried a different word. "—strangers."

"No," Wilber said sadly. "We're a bit different. But we can help you. Wait here."

The human nodded.

—

"Wilber, what are we doing?" Orville asked.

They were hiking back out of the woods and toward the village, but that obviously wasn't what Orville meant. "You mean, why are we helping that . . . what was it? That human?"

"Yeah, we could get in big trouble," Orville said. "I mean really big trouble. We could get banished."

Wilber nodded. He hadn't been exaggerating when he said the others of his species would probably throw rocks at an alien. Especially one as bizarre looking as that human. The Hodarii weren't a violent species, but they were suspicious of anything foreign to their own experience. Wilber's father knew that better than anyone.

But Wilber was willing to take the risk. "Someone's got to help him, Orville. And truthfully, banishment doesn't scare me all that much."

Orville sulked for a short time as they continued to walk. Finally he said, "Okay, I'm with you, Wilber."

The sound of engines filled the air, and instinctively the two Hodarii stepped aside. A moment later three all-terrain vehicles roared through the underbrush, passing them quickly. In the cabins, Wilber and Orville saw Hodarii wearing official uniforms and grim expressions.

"Uh-oh," Orville said, "It looks like our alien has already been discovered."

"Maybe not," Wilber replied. "That's a search team. They might just be looking around for the meteor site. But we'd better hurry."

The two Hodarii jogged back to the village and straight to Uncle Horis's oil factory. They ran inside and found themselves in a huge room where workers carefully watched and adjusted machines that pressed the bezza into a thick, goopy oil substance.

"Wilber!" Uncle Horis said, spotting them and walking over. The older Hodar was obviously delighted to see his nephew. He spoke loudly to be heard over the machines. "What a pleasant surprise. What can I do for you?"

"I . . ." Wilber said, biting his tongue as he forced himself to tell a lie. "I've decided to take you up on your offer to learn the bezza business. Do you think Orville and I could look around and maybe take some oil to study?"

"Of course!" Uncle Horis said, clapping his hands together so that his wings flapped. "Wonderful! Look around. The place is yours."

Wilber couldn't tell what stung him more: telling a lie or the false joy it gave his uncle. He promised he'd make amends as soon as he had helped the alien.

Meanwhile, he and Orville made a show of walking around and examining the machines. But as soon as Uncle Horis was distracted, they made straight for the storage rooms. There, cans of bezza oil were stacked floor to ceiling. Each Hodar took a can of oil and then bolted from the factory.

They sprinted through the village and down the path toward the forest. But they'd only gone a short distance when they noticed one of the all-terrain vehicles parked right across the trail. Two Hodar stood beside it, and one of them raised a winged arm as they approached.

"Sorry, egglets," he said. "We're closing down all the trails into the forest for a while."

Stiff as a board, Orville was too frightened to talk. But Wilber remained calm. "Why?" he asked innocently. "What's going on?"

"Nothing too interesting," the Hodar replied casually. "Just clearing some old brush to prevent forest fires this season."

"Oh," Wilber said. "We heard there was a meteor crash. We figured it had something to do with that."

The Hodar official tilted his beak down, a sign of consternation. Then he said, "Well, I'm not supposed to say, but you're right. We're just checking out the crash site to make sure it poses no danger. Things should be back to normal by tomorrow."

"So are there scientists and stuff in the forest already?" Wilber asked.

The Hodar started to look irritated. "Well, no. We're just closing things off. Researchers will be sent in as soon as they arrive. For right now, no one's allowed any farther than this."

"Oh, okay," Wilber said as casually as he could. "Thanks anyway."

Orville's feet seemed rooted into the ground, and Wilber had to practically pull him back along the trail. As soon as they were out of sight, they paused.

"Well, I guess that's it," Orville said. "There's nothing we can do now."

Wilber shook his head. "We've got to help him. If the Hodar find him—"

"Don't you think they already have?" Orville said.

"No way. Trust me, they don't want to admit to anything that could shatter their assumptions. If they saw anything at all, they pulled back and are going to close down the place until they figure out what to do. Which means that alien is still in there somewhere, waiting for us. And maybe now he's scared."

Orville swallowed. "I guess you're right. But there's no way for us to reach him."

Wilber thought about it a moment. The paths were the only entry into the forest. The trees were too thick to try any other way. He knew of other hatchlings who'd gotten lost in the woods and never returned.

Out of habit from imagining his father's flying machines, Wilber glanced upward as he searched for an answer. His eyes fell instantly on the cliffs towering over them, the same cliffs that overlooked the alien's orb. Then he reached into his pocket and pulled out the note from his father, with the diagram attached.

"There is a way."

———

A short time later they were standing near the edge of the cliffs. Lengths of wood, cloth, and wire were scattered about Wilber's feet. The materials were easy enough to come by. Thanks to his uncle's manufacturing business, Wilber had been able to borrow supplies from several shops in town. He'd gotten everything his father recommended in his notes: lightweight wood; strong, thin wire; and cloth that was both lightweight and tear resistant. It was the same cloth that Uncle Horis's workers used to make bags to gather the bezza nuts.

Following his father's diagram, Wilber assembled three long poles into a triangle and lashed them together with wire. Then he used more wire to tie the canvas directly to the frame. Tearing off more strips of cloth, he constructed a sort of hanging seat for himself. The design was brilliantly simple, and in a short time Wilber had built a full-scale model of his father's gliding device.

"There," Wilber said at last. "Now, all I have to do is tie in another seat and—"

"Um, Wilber," Orville said. "I . . . I'm not going to do this with you."

Wilber looked at his friend, who couldn't meet his gaze. "You're not?"

"Look, you're my best friend, and you know I thought your dad was great before he got sent away but . . ." the young Hodar pointed to the cliffs. "It's a long way down."

Wilber felt bitterness rise in him, then subside. How could he blame Orville? It *was* a long way down.

"Okay," he said. "But I still need to build the other seat. To hold the oil cans."

Minutes later the glider was complete.

With Orville's help, Wilber hoisted it up. It was surprisingly easy to lift. The wood was very light, and the breeze that blew across the cliff tops seemed to tug at the cloth, minimizing the weight even more. As Orville held on, Wilber stepped into the sling that served as his seat. He adjusted his grip on the frame.

"Okay," he said. His heart started to beat rapidly. He had meant to say, "Okay, I'm ready," when he suddenly realized he wasn't.

He wasn't ready.

What if his father was wrong?

Suddenly, all the skeptical voices he'd ever heard began to shout loudly in his brain. He heard the protests of his uncle, the groans of his teachers, the jeers of his classmates—all of them telling him his father was crazy.

If his father was wrong, then Wilber was about to leap to his death.

But then Wilber remembered how much his father loved him. His father would never have sent him the diagram, the secret to building the device, if he wasn't convinced it would work.

In that moment, Wilber made his choice.

He charged forward into space.

Shutting his eyes tight, he reached the edge of the cliff and jumped. Instantly he dropped, feeling the sickening sensation of his stomach leaping up out of his body. But in the same moment he thought, *I'm falling,* he stopped falling. It was as if a giant hand snatched hold of the gliding device and was pushing it forward rather than pulling it down.

Terrified, Wilber forced open his eyes. The wind rushed against his face. Before him, the forest valley unfolded in all its green splendor. He looked down, hardly believing that his feet were off the ground. But they were.

He was flying.

The feeling was too great even for words. He was the first of his kind ever to fly. And his father was right.

For a few moments, Wilber just drifted, lost in joy over his success and pride in his father. But then he recalled his rescue mission. His first task was to practice maneuvering.

Wilber had memorized his father's directions in the diagram, and he gently tilted his weight to the left. Slowly the glider began to turn left. After a moment he shifted the other way, and the glider turned that way as well. It was easy!

Lifting his feet up caused the nose of his glider to tilt down. Instantly the glider began to drop . . . a little too fast. Thinking quickly, Wilber pulled his feet down. The nose lifted, the wind caught in the glider's cloth, and the device began to float level again.

Wilber was surprised at how swiftly he learned to steer the device. It was as if the instincts for flight were already in him, hidden somewhere, waiting to be unlocked by a single bold leap into the unknown. In a short time he was guiding the glider in any direction he willed, rising up or dropping down depending on how the glider caught the air currents. The movements felt more natural than walking.

The gleam of sunlight on the orb roused Wilber from his reverie. Somewhere down there the alien was waiting for him. Wilber began to spiral downward, always keeping the gleaming object in the center of his tightening circle.

His descent was no trouble at all. But as he reached the tree line he realized that he had no idea how to land—especially in a thicket of branches. He also didn't know how to stop. Flying high above the ground, he felt his speed to be slow and leisurely. But now as he closed in, gauging his pace by fixed objects on the ground, he realized he was hurtling forward. He banked left and right, but it didn't do any good. Steering wasn't the same as slowing.

At the last minute all he could do was clench his beak, shut his eyes, and hope.

He crashed into the branches and felt twigs snap against his face and arms. Something hard—a branch probably— struck him across the forehead and he gasped. A second later he came to an abrupt halt, tangled in the straps of his glider. He hung there for a moment, shaken, not knowing whether he should feel frightened or lucky to be alive.

He chose both and determined to get out of the contraption as soon as possible. But the cloth seat was too ensnared in branches and twigs for him to free himself.

Suddenly the alien appeared. It climbed trees as easily as Wilber had taken to flying. Pulling itself up onto a branch, it drew a small knife out of a pocket and sliced at the cloth. In moments, Wilber was free.

"Are you all right?" the human asked through its translating machine.

"Yeah, I think so." Wilber felt his forehead. Yellow blood streaked his finger tips, but the cut didn't appear too bad. "I . . . I brought your bezza oil."

The cans had been tossed from the glider in the crash, but together they found them.

"We have to hurry," the human said. "I heard vehicles approaching. They'll be coming soon."

"Yes, they're bringing in scientists."

"Will . . ." the alien hesitated. "Will they be friendly?"

"I don't think so," Wilber replied.

The human nodded. This didn't seem to surprise it. Wilber had the impression this creature had visited many alien planets.

Quickly the human took the two cans of oil back to the orb. Wilber wondered what it would do with them since the big silver ball didn't appear to have any openings. But when the alien touched a spot on the orb, a door popped open. Inside, Wilber could see a seat and all kinds of electronic devices.

"What is this thing?" he asked in amazement.

The human smiled. "My . . . glider."

Shouts drifted through the trees, followed by the roar of vehicle engines. The human picked up its pace. It pressed several buttons inside the orb, and another panel opened up on the vehicle's outer skin. Hurrying back outside, the human poured the bezza oil into the opening, sealed it up, then jumped back into the device. The creature next studied several lights on the control panel, then nodded in satisfaction.

"Like water to a thirsty man," it said.

"What?" Wilber asked.

The cries of alarm were closer now. The Hodarii officials would arrive any minute.

The human showed its teeth for the last time. "Thank you." It held out its strange, wingless limb. They clasped hands for a moment. Then the alien let go and motioned for Wilber to step back. With one final wave, the human pressed a button and the orb sealed itself shut, looking seamless once more. A second later it began to rumble and whine. Wilber took a few more steps back, then scrambled up the slope as the ground began to quake.

As he reached the edge of the crater, the orb began to lift itself out of the hole. Wilber was stunned. As impressed as he'd been with his father's invention, this was something centuries ahead of it. He could see no wings or lifting device of any kind. The orb appeared to raise off the ground effortlessly. It hovered in midair for a fraction of a second and then, with a sound of thunder and the speed of lightning, it flashed away into the sky.

Wilber was still standing there, reeling from the power and beauty of the thing he'd seen, when two Hodarii vehicles rolled up. He recognized the same Hodarii he'd spoken with before.

"What are you doing here?" the official demanded, but that question was quickly replaced by another. "Where is the orb we saw here earlier?"

Wilber pointed upward. "It flew away."

"Flew?" the official scoffed. "Nothing can fly. You'd better be careful before you get banished to the southern continent."

Wilber smiled. "You won't have to banish me. I'm going to the southern continent on my own."

The official looked at him as if he were crazy. "And just how do you plan to get there on your own?"

Wilber laughed. "I'm going to fly."